Gershwin

Gershwin

Ruth Leon

HAUS PUBLISHING • LONDON

First published in Great Britain in 2004 by
Haus Publishing Limited
26 Cadogan Court, Draycott Avenue
London SW3 3BX

A CIP catalogue record for this book is available from the British Library
ISBN 1-904341-23-3

Designed in Adobe InDesign by Rick Fawcett and typeset in Garamond 3
Printed and bound by Graphicom in Vicenza, Italy
Front cover: Lebrecht Music Collection
Back cover: Lebrecht Music Collection

Contents

Dedication   iv

Prelude: Our Love Is Here To Stay   1

Looking For a Boy 1898–1914   4

Soon 1914–1917   14

Bidin' My Time 1917–1920   21

Aren't You Kind of Glad We Did? 1920–1923   37

Rhapsody in Blue 1923–1925   47

Concerto in F 1925–1928   63

An American in Paris 1928–1929   86

Strike Up the Band 1929–1933   100

I Loves You, Porgy 1933–1935   118

Shall We Dance? 1935–1937   132

But Not For Me 1937   139

Chronology   150

Major Works   158

Picture Sources   161

Selected Songs   162

Index   164

Dedication

This book is for Edward Jablonski, who taught me everything I know about George Gershwin, everything, that is, that George didn't teach me himself through his music and his life.

Ed's friendship and dedication to 'getting it right' have been an inspiration and, Ed, whatever I've missed, or mistaken, or overlooked, or overemphasised, is my fault and not yours. You've been the best mentor and one-man cheering section any writer could possibly have. You have allowed, even encouraged, me to plunder your books and corrected me when I've gone off the rails. Thank you.

When you wrote your great biography you thanked your friend and editor and said, 'I only hope it is worthy of the subject and of you.' I had the same hope, wanted to put the first published copy of this book into your hands, Ed. But then, on 10 February early this year, you went and died on me. What kind of comment was that? But this book is still for Edward Jablonski who will live as long as anyone writes about George Gershwin.

RUTH LEON

Prelude · Our Love is Here to Stay

'George Gershwin died on July 11, 1937, but I don't have to
believe it if I don't want to.'   JOHN O'HARA

In the scratchy newsreel all we can see at first is the back of a man
playing the piano. But the back is vibrating with pleasure; the
strong shoulders of a tall, impeccably tailored gent move animat-
edly to conduct the music as he plays, the rhythm of the music
obviously infectious even without our hearing a sound. Then the
head turns, and a strong Semitic face with a receding hairline
grins as he catches sight of what's behind him, a line of chorus
girls dancing to the sound of his impromptu concert.

It's a rehearsal for *Strike Up The Band* and George Gershwin is
playing for fun, exulting at being part of the madhouse that is
a Broadway musical in the early stages of rehearsal. Or maybe
he saw something in the choreography that made him want to
correct the tempo. No one knows, but this perfectly captured
moment, shown me by the immensely gracious author of the
Ur-text Gershwin biography, Edward Jablonski, is what made
me first want to learn more and finally write about George
Gershwin.

In it a man, still young, at the height of his fame and powers,
is enjoying himself hugely. This man composed *Strike Up the
Band* and 27 other Broadway shows, 4 film musicals, one opera
of genius, *Porgy and Bess,* 20 works for the concert hall including
Rhapsody in Blue, one of the most enduring of American compositions, as well as some 387 of the most beautiful and frequently

performed individual songs of the Golden Age of American songwriting, at least 50 of which have become standards.

In every one of his works, whether song or show or concert piece, you can hear all the elements that he heard in his New York youth – the kletzmer and folk music of the Lower East Side, the Western European classics of mid-town concert halls, and the jazz and blues of Harlem – all synthesized into a sound that is rich and varied and uniquely Gershwin.

He travelled widely, made love to many women, among whom were some of the most beautiful and accomplished of his age, invented The Jazz Age (with the novelist F Scott Fitzgerald, who named it), and personified the glamour and excitement of New York, giving the city a sparkle it retains to this day.

George was interested in all the latest innovations, including interior design (his homes were always the 'latest thing' and he set a trend in the use of colour and fabric) and painting (much more than a Sunday painter, Gershwin's works in oil are of professional standard), but his real genius was for encapsulating his life and times into his music. While never patronizing his audience, he had the gift of composing music to which it could relate, could understand both at the immediate level of 'nice tunes' and at the more profound, even spiritual, level of the catch at the heart of a really good song.

George Gershwin made the most of every moment of his happy, productive and charmed life. He had to—he didn't know it, but he would be dead of a brain tumour before his 39th birthday. Every time I look at that scrap of newsreel, see that animated back dancing at the keyboard, watch that flirtatious, charming young man loving his life and believing his luck, and every time I hear someone sing 'Embraceable You,' 'Swanee,' or 'I got Rhythm,' or play 'Rhapsody in Blue,' Fascinating Rhythm,' or the 'Concerto in F,' George is right there with me. And with all of us.

And that is what this book is about.

GEORGE GERSHWIN

1898 - 1937
Compositeur Américain

Looking For a Boy · 1898 -1914

She's what Mammy writers write about, and what Mammy singers sing about. But they don't mean it and I do.

GEORGE GERSHWIN ON HIS MOTHER

Rose Bruskin was a beauty. The daughter of a prosperous St Petersburg furrier, she was 16 when she met 21-year-old Morris Gershovitz and he fell deeply in love with her, although marriage had to wait until both families had emigrated to New York. Unlike most Jews in Tsarist Russia, their families had neither been confined to the urban ghettos or rural shtetls nor subjected to the periodic pogroms in which Cossacks, unrestrained – indeed encouraged – by the law, whipped, shot or otherwise disposed of any available Jew. Nonetheless, both the Bruskins and the Gershovitzs realized the better part of valour was exile and followed friends and family to the Lower East Side. By the time they all arrived, Rose was 19 and Morris 24, and the couple finally married in July 1895.

In Russia, Morris had worked his way up to foreman in a shoe factory and, as a skilled leather worker, he had no trouble finding a job in New York, which made Rose and Morris Gershovitz – or Gershvin as they were soon styling themselves – a cut above most of the 1.5 million Russian Jewish immigrants who flooded the streets of the Lower East Side in the latter years of the 19th century. Most joined the general mass of street traders and sweatshop workers living in wretched tenements, intent only on finding a better life for their children. Rose and Morris lived in a pleasant flat above a shop on the corner of Hester and Eldridge Streets and, with Morris in regular employment, there was always money to feed, clothe and educate their growing family.

Their first child, Israel, known as Isadore or Izzy and later world-famous as Ira, was born in 1896 at the Hester Street flat. Shortly thereafter Morris was offered a job in Brooklyn so the family moved to a rather prepossessing mansion in a tree-lined street known as 242 Snedicker Avenue. Perhaps in response to the newfound leafy hedge-lined grandeur, the Gershvins temporarily became the Gershwines.

Morris changed jobs often and, since he liked to walk to work, the family was constantly on the move. Their fortunes waxed and waned, particularly after Morris went into business for himself. He was an easy-going man, gentle and philosophical, who seemed unconcerned by the success or failure of his various business

New arrivals from old Europe are processed through the immigration halls at Ellis Island

ventures so long as he could listen to operas on his brand new phonograph and avoid the sharp side of Rose's tongue.

Rose had a very different personality: highly strung and determined that her children should have the education she lacked. That way, she reasoned, if they failed at the other professions, they could always be teachers. Music seemed to her a waste of time and formed no part of her plans. George later described her as *'nervous, ambitious and purposeful'* and said, with no apparent self-pity, that she hadn't been a doting or even a particularly attentive mother,

George Gershwin's mother Rose

although he had always been aware of her ambitions for him and her disappointment when he wouldn't or couldn't follow her pre-ordained plan. Even when he had become a star she often criticized or interfered.

Rose was quick to judge her children as they grew up, but she knew how to have fun too. Among Ira's childhood moneymaking schemes were providing the food and cards for her weekly all-female poker games and accompanying her on occasional forays to the racetrack. During the early days her primary concern was making sure Morris wasn't 'losing his shirt' on each successive business and she kept the books for most of the string of enterprises in which he became embroiled. At various times he owned or part-owned a bakery, a Turkish bath, a small chain of restaurants, and a pool parlour. He was even, briefly and disastrously, a bookie at Brighton Beach Race Track. When she was unable to stop him 'going off the rails', she would pawn her diamond ring until his next venture rescued their finances and she was able to retrieve it.

Jacob Gershwine, for that is the name on George Gershwin's birth certificate, was born during the family's Brooklyn sojourn in Snedicker Avenue on 26 September 1898. The date his name became George is buried in the mist of time since his younger sister Frances said that she could never remember his being called anything else. His birth was followed quite soon by Arthur's in 1900 and the family was completed by the arrival of Frances in 1906.

George was a hyperactive little boy, not scholarly and calm like Ira, but the two brothers had, from childhood, an almost mystical connection. George admired his older brother and wanted to be more like him. His interest in painting and, later, literature was certainly due to Ira's influence and although he suffered a setback when an insensitive teacher laughed at one of his efforts in front of his entire class, he persevered and he continued to draw and paint throughout his life.

Music was, however, a different matter: an interest that was entirely his and to which he came by himself. At the age of 10 he refused to go to a violin recital in the school auditorium by an 8-year-old schoolmate, Max Rosenzweig, later the international virtuoso, Max Rosen. But, as he played outside, his senses were unexpectedly assaulted by the sound of Rosenzweig playing Dvořák's *Humoresque.* He *had* to meet the boy who was creating this magical sound but he was afraid to draw attention to his absence by returning to the school hall. Although it started to pour with rain, he waited outside until he thought it was safe to enter. But by that time Maxie had left. Soaking wet, George followed him home. *From the first moment we became the closest of friends,* he said later.

The two boys did everything together in spite of Max's family living on the Upper West Side and the Gershwines being constantly on the move. George persuaded Max to play truant with him and the two boys roamed around Manhattan listening to all kinds of music. They wrestled, (*I always threw him,* boasted George) and they'd talk endlessly about music. Max was George's introduction into a more cultured world and they remained friends until Max began to play in public. The reason that they drifted out of each other's lives is unclear but it may have been because Max told George he wasn't good enough to accompany Max's violin playing, told him he 'didn't have it in him'. Furious, George ingratiated himself with one of his playmates whose family had a piano and he taught himself to play the music he heard around him on the streets.

His aunt, Kate Bruskin Wolpin, had attempted to teach him the rudiments of formal piano technique from about the age of 11, although Ira, with his dogged commitment to learning, had made better progress. But surprisingly, it was the social-climbing Rose who would give George, then about 12, his best ever present. His mother, feeling that her sister's house was more refined because her front room had a piano, bought one. Ira recalled, 'No sooner had the upright been lifted through the window of the front room than George sat down and played a popular tune of the day. I remember being particularly impressed by his left hand. I had no idea he could play.' Neither of course, did Rose, but she soon worked out that, if her wayward second son could be made more presentable and persuaded to play for her friends, it would be worth her while to encourage this interest until she could settle on a respectable profession for him.

And so it began. But although the music he heard in his head and his struggle to find it on the piano gave George's life a structure he had never known before, it didn't stop him from being a tearaway. While a maid looked after the two younger children and

George, Ira and Arthur Gershwin with their cousin Rose

Ira was protected by his love of reading, George ran wild on the streets of Manhattan. He was a small, wiry boy, very quick and mischievous. He found his friends in whichever neighbourhood he happened to be in at the time, and together they tormented the local pushcart traders, fought, and generally made a nuisance of themselves. School held no attraction for this hyperactive child. Because of the family's frequent moves, George never spent long in any school and this contributed to his sense of rootlessness, as was common among the Eastern European immigrant Jews who teemed through the crowded concrete streets of the New York Jews. If George had not found music, he might easily have drifted into petty crime and teenage gangs.

Later in life the sounds he had heard in the crowded streets – the kletzmer bands of wandering clarinetists, the street singers with the latest popular songs, the young black tap dancers vying with each other for a few cents and the crowd's approval, the stew of immigrant folk music – would all be put to use in his songs and concert pieces, all become part of the unique mix which would be Gershwin.

In the early decades of the 20th century, until the invention and widespread use of air-conditioning, everyone who could afford to leave avoided the heat and humidity of New York in the summer. The colonies of Rhode Island and the Hamptons were not hospitable to Jews, so the more prosperous among them would escape to the Catskill Mountains where they built their own resorts – opulent hotels with famously lavish kosher food, and where the top-line entertainers performed alongside the young hopefuls who usually doubled as waiters.

In 1913, George got his first musical engagement. Every aspiring Jewish comic, singer, musician or actor from George Burns to Danny Kaye started in the Jewish holiday resorts in the Catskills Mountains, or 'The Bortsch Belt', as it was known, and George Gershwin was no exception. But, as usual with George, he did it younger than anyone else. In the summer of 1913, when he was 15, he became a relief pianist in the Catskills at a salary of $5 a week, more than many full-grown men working in factories. That financial potential, far more than any talent he might have possessed, persuaded his father to let him leave school and become a musician.

Rose arranged some 'proper' lessons for George. He had already outgrown his dear Aunt Kate and the local teacher, Miss Green, and was duly dispatched to a Hungarian bandleader, the impressively mustachioed Mr Goldfarb, who charged the hefty sum of $1.50 a lesson and *played the piano with great gusto and a barrel of gestures.* It was Goldfarb who, according to George, *started me on a book of excerpts from the grand operas,* (which must have been most gratifying to Morris) and six months later he had progressed as far as the Overture to *William Tell.*

Then came the next big step. He had made friends with a music student, Jack Miller, a few years older than George and pianist for the Beethoven Society Orchestra. Miller recommended him most highly to his own teacher, Charles Hambitzer, who had recently arrived in New York from Wisconsin and whom George was to call *the first great musical influence in my life.*

Hambitzer was an exceptional musician as well as an inspiring teacher. Good-looking, in his early 30s, an accomplished player of both string and percussion instruments, he was mild-mannered and much loved by his students. Nathaniel Shilkret, who became a respected music director for RKO Pictures, said of him: 'He was one of the greatest pianists I ever heard. And I would say he was a genius.' He taught George more than anything by example, playing the pieces and allowing George to find his way into them.

At his first meeting with George, Hambitzer listened sympathetically as George launched into the Overture from *William Tell,* complete with Goldfarb flourishes, and gently suggested that they go find Goldfarb and shoot him, 'and not with an apple on his head, either'. Nothing could have more endeared him to the boy than humour coupled with the solid but implicit musical criticism and Hambitzer became his regular teacher.

He found George a deeply committed student. He was well prepared and enthusiastic. He arrived early and always wanted to stay late. He absorbed all the music that Hambitzer threw at him from Liszt to Chopin to Debussy. At the same time he went to every concert he could, filling his scrapbooks with the programmes of the great visiting musicians playing the classical repertoire.

The relationship between Hambitzer and Gershwin was one of mutual respect and genuine affection. Hambitzer called George 'a genius' and was heard to opine that, 'he will make his mark in music if anyone will'. Although Hambitzer's later life was marked by the sorrow of the premature death of a much-loved young wife, alcoholism, and at least one nervous breakdown, he never showed anything but kindness to the rather difficult boy that Gershwin was when he first met him. While he certainly tamed him and channelled his enormous talent, he never tried to break him and he may have been the first adult who really loved him.

One area they disagreed about was popular music. With his infallible ear for what was 'hot', George had begun to listen to his slightly older contemporaries, such as Jerome Kern and Irving Berlin, whose first hit, 'Alexander's Ragtime Band' (1911), was all the rage. He asked Hambitzer to teach him about writing songs but his teacher wanted him to learn first about harmony and theory from the renowned teacher Edward Kilenyi. George was now surrounded by all kinds of musical influences, and music was the fulcrum of his life.

This made a great contrast with his schoolwork. At the High School of Commerce on the Upper West Side, the only bright spot of George's day was when he played the piano for morning

> 'I have a pupil who will make his mark in music if anybody will. The boy is a genius, without a doubt; he's just crazy about music and can't wait until it's time to take his lesson. No watching the clock for this boy! He wants to go in for this modern stuff, jazz and what not. But I'm not going to let him for a while. I'll see that he gets a firm foundation in the standard music first.'
>
> CHARLES HAMBITZER

assembly. He was bored and discouraged and his grades would not have allowed him to enter any kind of university, not even City College. Rose, who had decided that George was to be an accountant, was in despair. Morris, however, was relieved to discover that George possessed a talent of any kind, since he had from early childhood suspected (and unfortunately frequently said out loud) that his second son was going to be a 'bum'.

Given his fairly chaotic and unsupportive home life, George's music teachers and the friends he was beginning to make in popular music circles provided a kind of family warmth he needed. Much later George's friends would complain that he was at times very close, at others distant, but this had at least as much to do with his upbringing as with the conflict between his need for space in which to work and his desire always to be the centre of a group.

Edward Kilenyi

In 1914 two surprising events changed his direction. Charles Hambitzer's wife died, leaving him heartbroken and with a small daughter to support, which greatly curtailed his teaching activities in favour of more lucrative performing opportunities; and George was unexpectedly offered a job of which Hambitzer heartily disapproved.

Without hesitation, and with only token opposition from Rose and Morris, George walked out of the High School of Commerce in the middle of the spring semester of 1914 and never went back. He was now a professional musician.

Soon · 1914 - 1917

Tin Pan Alley was George Gershwin's destination and his destiny.
A block of West 28th Street between Fifth and Sixth Avenues, a
row of undistinguished houses most of which still stand today in
the heart of what is now New York's flower market, Tin Pan Alley
in 1914 was the centre of the popular music world. It had got its
nickname from the cacophony issuing from every room in every
house that could be heard from the street as song pluggers played
and sang their employers' wares.

A song plugger, in those days before widespread use of recorded sound, was the essential link between the composer and his
market, the singer-pianist who allowed potential customers to
hear the songs. The product sold by the publishers who had
their offices in Tin Pan Alley was sheet music, which enabled
both professionals and public to perform the song more or less
as written. Sheet music was an enormous business. This was an
age when there was a piano in all but the poorest front rooms;
vaudeville and the musical theatre flourished, with the plotless
song and dance shows known as revues on every corner. People
wanted to buy, from the publisher, the songs associated with
their favourite performers.

The competition was vicious. The publishers knew little or
nothing about the music they sold. Songwriters were ruth-
lessly exploited, paid a few cents to turn out what their masters
thought of as commercial fodder, and then set to work on formu-
la songs according to whatever had become this week's hit. So, if
it was 'mammy' songs (songs performed by white performers in

black face, about the nannies who had brought them up), ragtime parodies, Italian ballads or songs based on place names, that was what they had to write.

Into this sweatshop came George to play for Jerome H Remick & Company, one of the newer publishing houses. He had been introduced to the manager Mose Gumble, who was initially against hiring the 15-year old boy, until he heard him play and realized that his sight-reading skills were impeccable and more than compensated for his lack of experience. Gumble offered him $15 a week – a fortune for a green boy – in the 'professional department' both playing piano for song pluggers and demonstrating the songs for the potential customers. He was, in effect, a salesman. To offset his extreme youth, he

Gershwin dressed as a 'baby banker' during his years with Jerome H Remick and Company

came to work in a formal dark suit and high collar, looking more like a baby banker than a pianist.

Remick's was not as well established as other publishers like Witmarks or Harms or Von Tilzer, but it was perfectly respectable and possessed its own stable of hack songwriters whose newest work was piled onto the upright piano in George's cubicle. Ignoring the clamour all around, he had to play songs for potential customers who drifted from room to room and from house to house along Tin Pan Alley until they found something that took their fancy. Sometimes he went with one of the singers to demonstrate the songs out of town or at the theatres themselves; sometimes they sent him to play them in the five-and-dime stores which shifted vast quantities of sheet music and kept a piano in the shop for just such demonstrations. George soon began to add his own improvements to the songs, a practice seriously frowned upon at Remick's. He tried offering his employers some songs of his own but was firmly put in his place. 'You're a piano pounder,' Gumble told him. 'We've got writers and singers. You just play.' So he used the time to improve his piano technique.

As early as 1915, George took a shot at writing songs himself. His first effort, with lyrics by his friend Leonard Praskins, was entitled 'Since I Lost You', but his ambition outran his technical skill and his melody meandered into a key from which he couldn't retrieve it. But the following year his passion for ragtime (and Berlin's success with 'Alexander's Ragtime Band') made the two of them try again and the result, 'Ragging the Traumerei', was at least complete, if not exactly singable.

George survived on little sleep. When he wasn't working for Remick's he was taking the train to Perfection Studios in East Orange, New Jersey, on Saturdays to lay down piano rolls for the Pianola automatic pianos. Perfection picked out in advance the short pieces they could sell. George, as a good sight-reader, did his best but these rolls were a mechanical way to enable those who couldn't play an instrument to have music in their homes. Each roll was 2 to 3 minutes long and George was initially paid $25 for 6 rolls, which he could easily cut in a single Saturday. To keep himself amused he often embellished. Until about 1920 the rolls were nearly always of someone else's music, although he did manage to slip in a few of his early works such as *Rialto Ripples,* which has the distinction of being his first published instrumental piece, and 'When You Want 'Em You Can't Get 'Em', his first published song. At some point, while Perfection were using several different names to make it look as though they had many pianists cutting their piano rolls for them, George finally decided on the spelling for his last name.

Fred and Adele Astaire in 1926

These Saturday afternoons had a real influence on the unique playing style that created such a stir at the fashionable parties he would later dominate. Elements of a staccato, bouncy Pianola style crept into George's performances and he would often play his own tunes in an offhand, almost throwaway style or in a completely unsuitable tempo. It was as though he was seeing the notation on the side of the piano roll box advising the customer to crank the Pianola at different speeds for different effects: 'Play at 80 for listening', 'Play at 100 for dancing'.

When not working at Remick's or making piano rolls, he was sneaking into performances in the mid-town concert halls after the intermissions when the ushers weren't so vigilant about tickets. And when not doing that, he was writing his own music.

One cold afternoon in 1915, a very slight young song-and-

Irving Berlin was born Israel Baline, 11 May 1888. 'Alexander's Ragtime Band' (1911) was the first of a string of hits, which included the unofficial American national anthem 'God Bless America', the theatrical anthem 'There's No Business Like Show Business' and the perennial favourite 'White Christmas'. His shows included *Annie Get Your Gun* and *Call Me Madam.* One of the first songwriters to produce his own shows, Berlin ran a publishing company and owned the Music Box Theatre. He never learned to read or write music and could play only in one key, F-sharp, and only on the black notes. He worked on a specially built piano that changed keys for him. He died in 1989, aged 101.

dance man and his sister came in to Remick's looking for some songs that would precipitate their move out of vaudeville and into the legitimate musical theatre. In the course of a long afternoon the two boys became fast friends and after trying all Remick's songs, they even swapped roles so that the dancer played the piano and the pianist tried dancing to his accompaniment. 'Wouldn't it be great if I could write a musical show and you could be in it?' said a 17-year old George Gershwin to a 16-year-old Fred Astaire. Not many years later, he did exactly that.

Home for the Gershvins by this time was up on 110th Street. The atmosphere at home remained cool. As always, George found warmth elsewhere, often with his uptown neighbours, Remick's composer Herman Paley and his brother Lou. Herman had met George at work and decided that he was a pianistic genius. He sought him out and took him home to meet his schoolteacher brother, who immediately succumbed to his charm. From then on George had a second family, more loving and concerned with him than the first. The Paleys' big, noisy artistic family provided a constant stimulus to George's inquiring young mind. His new friends pointed him towards books to read, music to listen to, and pianos to play in front of people who would admire.

George made several good friends during his time at Remick's, who remained in his closest circle until his death, including Irving Caesar, the lyricist of his first big hit, 'Swanee'. He admired various black musicians, including the arranger, Will Vodery, who became one of his sternest critics in the popular music field. But the job itself was arduous and boring, the money was less attractive to an 18-year-old virtuoso than it had been for a 15-year-old tyro, and he really wanted to write his own songs, not endlessly recycle those of others.

He was briefly tempted by a job offer from Irving Berlin, which paid a princely $100 a week. Berlin couldn't write musical notation, couldn't play in any key but F-sharp, had no knowledge of harmony or theory and therefore needed someone else to write down his songs. But Berlin had the honesty to tell him: 'If you worked for me you might start writing in my style and yours would become cramped.' 'You are too talented to be an arranger and a secretary,' Berlin added. 'You are meant for big things.'

While he was struggling through his Tin Pan Alley apprenticeship, his brother Isidore, now known as Ira, scraped though his graduation from Townsend Harris Hall and into a place at City College, which, surprisingly in view of his scholarly disposition, he hated. He stuck it out for less than two years, kept failing the maths requirements, and quit, but not before he made one of the most important friendships of his lifetime, with his namesake on the school newspaper, also an Isidore, last name Hochberg, who became the lyricist Yip Harburg and had the same kind of influence on Ira that Ira himself had on George.

When it became clear that Mose Gumble did not consider his young piano pounder as a major new composer, George tried Remick's competitors. The first to find a home was 'When You Want 'Em You Can't Get 'Em' which had lyrics by another Tin Pan Alley friend, Murray Roth. Sophie Tucker, the great vaudevillian, heard the song, liked its syncopation and catchy tune, and recommended it to the publisher Harry von Tilzer, who offered the boys $15 each for all rights. Murray took it, but George, ever the gambler, took an advance of $5 and held out for royalties. It never made any, but George Gershwin had made the leap to being a published songwriter.

From the first revues and musicals, a practice had grown up known as 'interpolation'. Established composers would often need one or two extra numbers and these gave opportunities to young songwriters such as Kern and Berlin, and now Gershwin, to gain both experience and attention by inserting songs into a Broadway show.

George and Murray, much cheered by the success (albeit not commercial) of 'When You Want 'Em You Can't Get 'Em', went on writing songs together and, on hearing that Sigmund Romberg was writing a big new show, took him 'My Runaway Girl' for possible interpolation. While underwhelmed by their song, Romberg liked and was amused by the two earnest young men and would always see George when he came back with his songs. He finally gave George his chance by choosing one of his tunes with a lyric not by Murray but by Harold Atterbury, Romberg's own lyricist, which became 'My Runaway Girl' and was included in *The Passing Show of 1916,* which opened at the Winter Garden on 22 June of that year. Buried as it was in a score that consisted of more than a dozen other numbers, all by Romberg, it passed without notice, but he was now a composer for the musical theatre.

One more first for him. Although it was not to be recorded for another 40 years, the undistinguished little rag *Rialto Ripples* that George had cut into a piano roll was bought for publication by none other than Remick's. In one year, he had had his first song accepted for publication, sold his first instrumental, and had his first theatrical outing.

There was little or no doubt about it, George Gershwin was on his way.

Bidin' My Time · 1917 -1920

Nobody expected me to compose music. I just did.

GEORGE GERSHWIN

In May 1917 George felt the walls of his cubicle in Tin Pan Alley were closing in. At nearly 19 and after more than two years as a piano pounder, George was anxious to move on. His experience with Romberg had made him keen to try his luck in the theatre. On an impulse, he gave Mose Gumble his notice to quit without having any idea as to how he was going to make a living. He consulted Will Vodery, who knew of a job, just vacated by Chico Marx, at a vaudeville theatre on 14th Street. Fox's City Theatre had its own orchestra but its performances were continuous so there had to be a staff pianist to accompany the acts during the orchestra breaks. George took the job, at $25 a week.

On his first evening, George arrived at work full of confidence but realised, after the first few songs, that the music he was handed wasn't standard material but specially written for the acts. There was no time to rehearse or even to read it through, and he got further and further out of step with the performers until he found that he was playing one song and they were singing another. Thoroughly humiliated, he stopped playing and the act finished unaccompanied.

The comic who followed made fun of his gaffe, drawing loud laughter from the audience and the other performers. When he pointed at George, shouting, 'Who told you you were a piano player? You ought to be banging the drums!', George could stand it no longer. He picked up his hat (but not his paycheque) and fled from the theatre, never to return. The sense of humour that he often in later life directed at himself, never extended to this incident. Years later, he would gaze into space and tell his companion, *The whole experience left a scar on my memory.*

Jerome Kern (1885-1945) was, like Irving Berlin, a good businessman. He wrote with some 21 different lyricists but all his songs have the same lyrical and musical sweetness. His 'All The Things You Are' is one of the most-recorded songs ever written, second only to Berlin's 'White Christmas'. His songs formed the backbone of the Astaire/Rogers movies and include 'I Won't Dance'. His shows include the groundbreaking 1927 *Show Boat*, which changed the face of the musical theatre, plus some 40 others. He told his daughter that his favourite song was 'Why Was I Born?' Like Berlin, Kern was a taciturn man whose joy was channelled entirely into the joyous music he wrote.

The Fox Theatre incident, though mercifully brief, was a horrible experience for one whose self-esteem had been entirely based on his musical abilities. As he saw it, his life to this point had been a litany of failures and disappointments: a disastrous educational career; a mother who was constantly disappointed in him; a father convinced he was going to be a 'bum'; the chilly atmosphere of his parents' dysfunctional marriage; the suffocating job at Remick's; and the constantly changing landscape of houses and apartments none of which ever became home.

He was, however, young and the young recuperate fast. George was now hired as rehearsal pianist and vocal coach on a new show. This was *Miss 1917,* with music by Victor Herbert and Jerome Kern and a book by P G Wodehouse and Guy Bolton. Victor Herbert was the most important and successful composer of operetta of his day, but it was his idol Jerome Kern whom George was most excited to meet. George loved his job, rehearsing the principals, coaching the chorus and ensemble, and entertaining the cast in the breaks.

Gershwin's friends and collaborators Oscar Hammerstein, Jerome Kern and Flo Ziegfeld

It included Vivienne Segal, Irene Castle, George White, and Marion Davies (later William Randolph Hearst's mistress). The team of producers was almost as celebrated, including Charles Dillingham and Florenz Ziegfeld. The sets were by Joseph Urban, the dances by Adolph Bohm. The entire team represented the cream of Broadway in the second decade of the 20th century.

Nevertheless, the show was a flop, running only a month, now completely forgotten. George, however, had the time of his life. Everybody loved him. He was surrounded day and night by theatre folk. The chorus girls were pretty. The work was interesting. And everyone he met on *Miss 1917* was to play a part in his theatrical future.

There is a story that Jerome Kern, hearing George improvise to amuse the cast after rehearsals, brought his wife Eva the following day expressly to meet 'this young man who is surely going to go places'. He offered to use his influence on George's behalf whenever he was ready to write his own show. Since Kern was not an especially warm man, his affection for the younger man was that much more remarkable.

Vivienne Segal, who would become the biggest musical comedy star on Broadway, sang two of George's songs at the regular Century Theatre Sunday night concerts. One, with the wonderful title of 'You-oo Just You' was bought by a Remick's representative and published in 1918 with Segal's picture on the cover.

'You-oo Just You', though, had a greater significance. It brought George together professionally for the first time with his close friend Irving Caesar, who wrote the lyric. Caesar used to drop into Remick's to hear George play when trying to sell his lyrics in Tin Pan Alley. By day Caesar was working as a mechanic in a car factory because his mentor, Henry Ford, deemed it necessary experience before he could run one of the Ford Motors divisions, an ambition Caesar himself didn't share. His one desire was to write songs. He and George wrote everywhere – in the billiard hall, on the bus, in the restaurant they went to on Sunday nights, even in the theatre, whenever they could scrounge tickets, or on the steps of the 56th Street entrance of Carnegie Hall before sneaking into a concert. Only after their first big hit did Irving quit his job at Ford.

George now had a wide circle of friends, centring on the Paley household, which included a large group of young people – Groucho Marx among them. George had a habit of heading for the piano as soon as he arrived or, at least, as soon as he was asked. He would play for hours, invariably his own music, to crowds of appreciative fans. A popular story of that time tells of his sitting with a pretty showgirl on his lap. Someone asked him to play and he rose with such alacrity that the girl ended up in a heap on the floor. He had already acquired his taste for beautiful women, late nights, champagne, and the other good things of life.

George, however, was fiercely ambitious and he let none of his pastimes interfere with his career. 'George had such drive and he tried to move so fast, that he left the rest of us far behind,' was the opinion of a friend from those days. He went on working as a rehearsal pianist for Jerome Kern, moving on to *Rock-a-Bye Baby* early in 1918.

A first big break came with George White's Scandals

There were two other significant consequences from what was (for George) the hugely successful flop of *Miss 1917*. The dancer George White remembered the young musician who had coached him and when he became the producer of the *George White Scandals,* he offered George Gershwin his first major show. And the company manager, Harry Askin, introduced him to the most powerful publisher on Tin Pan Alley, the formidable Max Dreyfus of T B Harms. When George first walked into Dreyfus's office at Harms the publisher was familiar neither with his few publications to date, nor with his reputation as a formidable pianist. It would seem that he simply liked him and his power was such that this liking alone gave George the necessary break.

Dreyfus made an important decision. 'He was the kind of man I like to gamble on,' he said later, 'and I decided to gamble.' He offered George $35 a week for nothing more than the right of first refusal on all his songs. For those he published, he would give George an advance of $50 and a royalty of three cents a copy. With this leap of faith began an association that would yield millions for both men. Buoyed by the prestige of a major publisher, George moved up several rungs on the professional ladder and for most of the rest of his life, Harms was George's exclusive publisher. Throughout his life, Dreyfus was to be standing in the shadows with wise and valuable advice. But, as Dreyfus was modest enough to note after George's death, 'A man with Gershwin's talent did not need anybody to push him ahead. His talent did all the pushing.'

Dreyfus wasn't infallible. When a shady producer, Edward B Perkins, announced *Half-Past Eight,* a new revue complete with bicycle acts and a huge African-American band led by James Europe, Dreyfus invested heavily, thinking it would launch George's theatrical career. George Gershwin was the name on the five new numbers and the show opened in Syracuse, New York on Monday, 9 December, 1918. It closed in Syracuse, New York, five days later, after one of those wonderful muddles that only the early theatre can offer. George barely scraped the fare home and said he never wanted to leave Manhattan again. He was, however, thrilled to have seen, for the first time, a poster bearing the legend 'Music by George Gershwin' outside a professional theatre.

The producer of *Half-Past Eight* ran out of money during the rehearsals and, not daring to ask Dreyfus or any of his other backers for more, decided to economise by dispensing with a chorus line. George, thinking he was being helpful, suggested that they fake a chorus line (in those days an essential requirement of any show) by using the male performers wearing Chinese pyjamas and covering their faces with Chinese umbrellas. On opening night three of the umbrellas wouldn't open, inevitably exposing the whiskers and beards of the 'girls' to the unintended hilarity of the audience and the fury of the *Variety* critic: '[this] two-dollar show isn't worth even the war tax,' he sniffed. (The war tax was a mere 40 cents.)

Now, at something of a loose end and broke, George was hired by Nora Bayes, a big Broadway star, to accompany her when she went on the road with a new revue, *Ladies First.* She interpolated two of George's songs, 'Some Wonderful Sort of Someone' and later 'The Real American Folk Song (is a Rag)' into the show but Nora and George didn't work well together. He was young and probably brash, refusing point-blank to change the ending of one of his songs for her. Miss Bayes was a star, used to getting her own way, and pointed out, not quietly, that both Berlin and Kern had accommodated her wishes. Their partnership did not last for more than the planned six-week tour of *Ladies First,* but it had one positive outcome.

When *Ladies First* reached Pittsburgh, a 12-year-old Oscar Levant, later pianist, composer and movie star, saw it and knew immediately that this Gershwin fellow playing for Nora Bayes was the real thing. In his autobiography, he wrote, 'I had never before heard such a brisk, unstudied, completely free and inventive playing.' He vowed there and then to hitch his star to Gershwin's, although George was, of course, unaware of it.

During the tour, two other George Gershwin songs were added to Miss Bayes' repertoire. 'The Real American Folk Song (is a Rag)' is a remarkable link, musically and lyrically, between the black Cakewalk music of the turn of the century, out of which the new ragtime had grown, and the predominantly white and Jewish theatre music that would be personified by the Gershwin brothers.

'The Real American Folksong (is a Rag)', a fine slow drag (a syncopated black dance rhythm) with a complex – but not overly complex – rhythmic sense, is the first of George's songs to be original and lasting. It is easy to sing, and perfectly apes several of the key elements in other popular songs. It's professional, bright, and tailored to its market. And it had lyrics from one Arthur Francis, a corruption of the names of both of George's younger siblings. This was Ira's pen name, chosen with characteristic modesty because he didn't want to be seen to cash in on his brother's embryonic success. 'The Real American Folksong (is a Rag)' was the first of their joint efforts to end up in a show.

Having returned to interpolating songs into the shows of others, George anonymously entered 'O Land Of Mine, America' for a New York newspaper's contest to find a new national anthem. This received a $50 runner-up award, which George shared with the lyricist, and was promptly forgotten.

'Play the tune that smells like an onion.' ALEX AARONS

Early in 1919 George was introduced to Alex, the son of the major Broadway producer, Alfred Aarons. It was just what Gershwin had hoped. *Every career needs a lucky break to start it on its way and . . . Alex Aarons decided to engage me as composer for his first show,* La-La-Lucille! *This was very brave of him because I was quite inexperienced at the time, never having written a complete score.* His father, Alfred, who was much more conservative, had originally thought of Victor Herbert to write the music but Alex loved unusual harmonies and unexpected melodies. Ira wrote that Alex was quite familiar with George's songs, even several as yet incomplete. 'Whisking his hand across George's shoulder, he would say: "Play me the one that goes like *that.*" Or: "Play the tune that smells like an onion." Or: "*You* know, the one that reminds

From the late 17th century, the slaves imported from Africa to work the cotton and tobacco plantations in the South brought their own diverse rhythms, depending on which part of Africa they came from. This music was not written down but was stamped, clapped, sung and 'shouted', a rhythmic form of religious polyphonal spiritual singing. Ragtime, a syncopated rhythm with the emphasis on the 'wrong' beat was an outgrowth of one of these traditions, as was Blues. Field worksongs – usually call and response – were adapted to spirituals.

me of the Staten Island ferry.'" Ira said George always knew which song he meant.

Alex had the sense to surround his new composer with a far more experienced team, particularly the lyricist Buddy DeSylva, who was a few years older than George. He was as brash, ambitious and hardworking as George himself but already had several hits behinds him. He and Arthur Jackson wrote the lyrics for most of the songs in *La-La Lucille* specifically but there were also a number of 'trunk' songs, songs which aren't used when they are written but are fished out of the 'trunk' later when a song is needed in a hurry.

Jerome Kern, on whom Gershwin had modelled his style, the first of the heavy-hitters to

The Cakewalk came from slaves mimicking the affected walks of their owners, limp wrists flapping, heads high, backs inclined backwards. By the early 19th century, by which time there were large communities of urban slaves working in domestic service in New Orleans, for example, slave dances on Sundays were a regular feature of life. Instrumental ragtime began to be written and played on pianos and other instruments, cakewalks developed into a tapping of the feet on the pavement (tap-dancing, for nearly a century practiced exclusively by blacks), Blues became a secular version of the religious songs from the plantation and Jazz developed in varying ways throughout the South, then followed the freed slaves North to Chicago and the other major cities.

support him, and the first to offer his help in the event that he decided to try for a show of his own, felt snubbed when George signed with Alex Aarons for *La-La Lucille* without even discussing it with him. According to Gerald Bordman, Kern's biographer, 'For several years thereafter he was noticeably cool towards George.' Ira always said that George hadn't spoken to Kern about *La-La Lucille* because, although he had kindly offered to interpolate one or two of his own songs into any show George was writing, Aarons decided that it had to be an all-Gershwin score and George didn't want to offend his mentor by rejecting his songs.

Only one song from *La-La Lucille* is still performed today, 'Nobody But You', but Max Dreyfus liked the songs well enough to publish seven of them. The score received little notice from the critics, although J B Atkinson (later Brooks Atkinson, the influential critic of the *New York Times*) who saw the show in its Boston tryout, found the music 'harmoniously pleasing', a comment which George, having abandoned his childhood scrapbooks, filed away as his first positive review.

The show – a musical about a couple who have to divorce in order to inherit – did well enough. It opened on the road in May, came into town in June, survived the summer heat and was only closed by an Actor's Equity strike in August. It wasn't a big hit, but neither was it a flop and it was George's first success as the composer of a whole show.

1919 was proving a banner year for other reasons too. In October the luxurious new Capitol Theatre opened on Broadway at 51st Street. The Capitol was the largest movie theatre in the world, complete with a full-size vaudeville stage, and its first attractions were Douglas Fairbanks' silent movie, *His Majesty the American,* and *Demi-Tasse,* an elaborate revue with a huge orchestra, many acts, and dozens of dancers whose shoes were fitted with tiny electric light bulbs. In the lobby, copies of the sheet music were displayed, much as CDs of the original cast albums are today, so the audience could buy them on the way out. The show was hugely successful and George had two songs in it. One, 'Come to the Moon', with lyrics by Lou Paley, was charming enough, but the other was to make his fortune.

Months earlier, during one of their regular meals at Dinty Moore's chop house in Times Square, Irving Caesar and George Gershwin had been discussing one of their favourite topics: how they could write a song that would catapult them into the upper reaches of Tin Pan Alley.

George knew only too well from his days in the cubicle at

Remick's that the moment a song became a hit, the publishers would promptly commission many more exactly like it. Currently in vogue were neo-orientalism, the use of place names as titles, Mammy songs, Americana, and one-step rhythms. Look at the huge hit 'Hindustan', they reasoned, a one-step with an exotic locale in the title, which yearned for home in the South. Why not write something with a one-step rhythm, but with an American placename instead of an oriental one, that borrows from American folk composer Stephen Foster (whose 'Swanee River' was a perennial favourite), and that any Mammy would be thrilled to have sung to her?

There and then, amid the detritus of a mid-town restaurant meal, these two Russian-Jewish boys, who had never been further from Times Square than Boston, started to sketch out the structure for a song for which they had no more aspiration than that it should resemble 'Hindustan' as closely as possible.

They continued working feverishly on the bus uptown towards the Gershwin home, then on 144th Street, but they weren't quite finished when they arrived. George's father Morris had a poker game going in the dining room with several of his cronies but that didn't stop George and Irving from noisily throwing notes and lines back and forth until, finally, they were satisfied.

More out of relief than anything else, Morris wrapped a piece of tissue paper around a comb, improvised an accompanying *obbligato,* and they all gave 'Swanee' its first performance. The following day, Irving dropped in on George while he was working as the rehearsal pianist on the *Ziegfeld Follies* and during a break they sang their new composition for the chorus girls. Caesar said, 'Girls always clustered around George when he played. Pianists used to be called piano pimps because women always clustered around them and no pianist had more women clustering around than George.' The *Follies* director, Ned Wayburn, caught the impromptu performance and was as impressed by the cast's reaction as by the song. He offered to include it in the opening show, which he was directing for the new Capitol Theatre.

Having sold their song, George and Irving promptly forgot about it until the opening nearly a year later. In the event, Wayburn did them proud. On a darkened stage, 'Swanee' was sung by Muriel DeForrest and the rest of the 60-strong cast, all tap-dancing (although the twinkling lights on their shoes were reserved for Gershwin and Caesar's other song 'Come to the Moon') and accompanied by an orchestra of 70. The audience applauded politely – by some accounts more than politely – but, despite George and Irving's enthusiastic selling of the sheet music in the lobby, ostentatiously buying it themselves to set what they hoped would be a good example, they sold scarcely any copies. Sales weren't any better in the music stores either. Irving was so discouraged that at one point George had to dissuade him from selling all the rights in his lyrics for $200.

They reckoned, however, without Buddy DeSylva, George's colleague on *La-La Lucille,* who had become a friend. DeSylva had been accompanist to Al Jolson, best known for his appearances in 'blackface' and called by Max Dreyfus, (who was not given to exaggeration), the 'most successful of all singers'. Jolson had been touring his show *Sinbad* around the country and had returned to New York briefly to star in one of the Winter Garden's Sunday Night concerts. DeSylva was invited to the party after the Sunday Night concert, and asked George to come with him.

Inevitably, George went straight to the piano, where he played a selection of his own songs, including the disappointingly received 'Swanee'. Jolson, perhaps the only singer of his day whose interest in a song could by itself guarantee a hit, loved it. What's more, he admired the oddity of its construction; the juxtaposition between the traditional 'Mammy' lyric, the driving momentum of the rhythms, the surprising key changes, and the way George 'sold' the song with his trademark player-piano staccato delivery. There and then Jolson decided to include it in the remainder of the *Sinbad* tour and, most significantly, to record it.

Al Jolson and 'Swanee' were a marriage made in heaven. George and Irving's song, with its mixture of sentimentality and genuine sentiment, commercial schmaltz and musical chutzpah, was a perfect match for Jolson's almost uncanny rapport with an audience that, in the aftermath of World War One, longed for home, any home, preferably the idealised Swanee River home of the song. Two Jewish boys from the Lower East Side of New York had caught the prevailing mood perfectly. A third, Jolson himself, knew how to make it universal.

Jolson recorded 'Swanee' on 8 January 1920 to instant acclaim. Dreyfus called it 'The Hit of Hits' and took a whole page in *Variety* to trumpet 'Al Jolson's Greatest Song'. He published the sheet music with Jolson's smiling face beaming from the cover. Both the recording and the sheet music sold in the millions and George's first year royalties reportedly amounted to more than $10,000. Within weeks the song had spread across the country and, with the recording, across the world. George would never again be anonymous or poor. He was just 21 years old.

In its way, 'Swanee' was an aberration in the Gershwin *oeuvre.* Although catchy and neatly phrased, it has little of the subtlety and delicacy

Al Jolson performing in the Jazz Singer

of most of George's other work. It is a stand-alone pop song, outside of a theatrical or film context, and has much in common with Stephen Sondheim's only stand-alone worldwide hit, 'Send In The Clowns', a song which, although it comes from the show *A Little Night Music,* was actually written as a solo for the leading lady who was complaining that she didn't have one, not because the show demanded it. What the two songs have in common is that neither composer ever again hit the charts (of sheet music sales, in Gershwin's time) with a stand-alone song and neither thought of himself as a pop songwriter. The hits concerned were almost accidental.

The irony, as Jablonski points out, is that it was 'Swanee', George's most obviously Tin Pan Alley song, that would take him out of 28th Street uptown into the Broadway theatre. If anything, it proved that he had learned the lessons of the previous five years – learned about the 'business' in 'show business', learned how to get himself and his work heard – and was ready to move from that Tin Pan Alley 'schoolroom' towards a wider world. George wanted not just to write for stars but to *be* both a star and a star-maker himself and the next step was to get himself a major Broadway show. 'Swanee' made it possible.

George seemed by now to have abandoned his original ambition to be a concert pianist, settling for what Noel Coward called 'the bitter palliative of commercial success'. His concert compositions were still under-developed. He had written 'Lullaby', a charming and elegant – albeit lightweight – string quartet. Although the death the previous year of his principal teacher, Charles Hambitzer, would have provided him with an excuse to give up concert music completely, he continued to study with his theory and harmony teacher, Kilenyi, and took a few lessons with the well-known Rubin Goldmark. George had little personal rapport with Goldmark, whose vanity caused problems when he announced that 'Lullaby', a piece that George had written before they had even met, clearly betrayed signs of his own influence.

People who didn't know George well often commented on his lack of formal musical training, fearing that without it he would produce nothing of lasting value. His friend the pianist Abram Chasins, a fellow student of Hambitzer's, castigated him on his reluctance to commit himself to a regular teacher and practice routine, and give up his profitable light music scribbling. Those who did know him well were aware that he had devised a course of study for himself, and that he had worked hard at listening to hundreds of serious concerts and later recordings, studying the scores of diverse composers, perfecting his pianistic dexterity, and, most importantly, actually *composing* all kinds of music. George Gershwin *had* committed himself to the formal study of music but, as usual, he had done so in his own way.

His performing skill was apparent, even at the crowded parties where he beat a path to the piano. Burton Lane, fellow Broadway composer, was fascinated by it: 'You could feel the electricity going through the room when he played. He could transpose into any key with the greatest of ease. He had total command of what he was doing. Musical surprises, unusual changes of keys. He was one of the few composers who had a real sense of humour.'

The sense of humour, in life and in music, was just what he needed for his first solo venture on Broadway. His friend George White, the dancer from *Miss 1917,* was about to set himself up in competition with the great impresario, Florenz Ziegfeld. Gershwin had been Ziegfeld's rehearsal pianist and therefore had a clear idea of the musical structure of these lavish, girl-driven shows. His worldwide hit 'Swanee' had given him credibility, and he brought with him the solid backing of Max Dreyfus and Harms, so he was now the perfect choice as sole composer of *The George White Scandals of 1920.* There had, indeed, been a *George White Scandals of 1919* that had opened the same week as *La-La Lucille,* but White was confident that he could improve on that score by Richard Whiting and Arthur Jackson, and Gershwin was confident that he was the man to do it.

Gershwin felt a revue-format show like George White's *Scandals* was the right showcase for his talents. As it turned out, he was correct, and although much of the music for that 1920 *Scandals* and, indeed, for the subsequent 1921, 1922, 1923, and 1924 editions was journeyman rather than brilliant, there were real pearls among the songs, even diamonds, and several – 'I'll Build a Stairway to Paradise', 'Somebody Loves Me' – have become standards. More importantly, George really began to learn with that first show how to write a musical from beginning to end, how to use the orchestra, how to showcase a star, and how to compose for a chorus often chosen far more for their looks than their singing or dancing.

Revues were enormously popular musical shows with no 'book' or story, consisting of songs, sketches, dances and production numbers – heavily populated spectacles which included singing, dancing, sets, costumes and a good deal of flesh. The many performers ranged from the most beautiful girls in town, who had little ability other than to look decorative, through a large chorus of dancers and singers, to the big stars of the time who each had a self-contained 'spot' on the bill to show off their wares. For many younger artistes – comics, singers and dancers – a job on a *Follies* or *Scandals* show was the passport to fame.

Most of George's songs came out of the notebooks he always carried and into which he wrote any scrap of tune, or even just an interesting modulation or key change. Only later, when he was writing for 'book' shows with a story and needed each song to take a specific place in the plot, did he start from scratch. But the five years of the *Scandals* completed his theatrical education while ensuring that his name was constantly up in lights on Broadway. He was still in his early 20s, young, elegant, good-looking, talented, sexy, and he had New York at his feet.

Aren't You Kind Of Glad We Did? · 1920 - 1923

'To me he was a celebrity already.'

IRA GERSHWIN

With the benefit of hindsight, the pairing of two devoted brothers – one a composer, the other a wordsmith – seems inevitable.
In the first decades of the 20th century it was anything but.
There was never any doubt, in his or in anyone else's mind, that
George's life was in music. For Ira, or Israel or Izzy or Iz, the path
was far less clear. By the early 1920s he had held a number of jobs
and never shown any affinity for any of them. Ira was as gentle
and modest as George was noisy and self-promoting. He was as
soft and round as George was tall and angular. He was bookish
where George was virtually uneducated. He was easily led by
those he loved, while George followed the drummer in his own
head. Ira was fussy, precise, almost prissy, whereas George skated
along just the right side of vulgarity. He became known as 'The
Jeweller' for his precision and as 'a hard man to get out of an easy
chair' for his love of family and home.

Sometimes George would take him to the Paleys' Saturday
evening parties and at one of them he met a vivacious young
relative of theirs, Leonore Strunsky. His perennial shyness was
such that it took him years to get to know her but, eventually,
she would persuade him into marriage.

Ira had loved words from an early age, written for a school
magazine, and, later, for anybody who would publish him,
for a while he had even been an unpaid vaudeville critic, and
even, occasionally, crafted a few undistinguished lyrics under

The ever popular George Gershwin reclines before the Paley family and friends. it was. it was

the name Arthur Francis. With characteristic modesty, he always basked in his brother's success without any hint of fraternal rivalry. 'I was new,' Ira wrote later. 'I didn't want to

there it was that Ira Gershwin met his future bride Lenore Strunsky.

trade on his name, even though he was my younger brother.'

As Ira became, in his quiet way, a member of the Paley set too, and met their friends and relatives, among whom he found Lenore, usually abbreviated to Lee, he became more confident about his lyrics and during the *Scandals* years there were several chances, still as Arthur Francis, to contribute the words to George's songs, sometimes with others. Ira's most successful pre-George partnership was with the composer Vincent Youmans, with whom he wrote *Two Little Girls In Blue*, a *bona fide* Broadway hit in 1921. Both he and Vincent were so young (Youmans was only 21, Ira 24) that the producer, Alex Aarons, who had given George his first show *La-La Lucille*, asked them to stay out of the way when the backers arrived in case they withdrew their $100,000 out of concern that the writers were just kids. The critics were kind, singling out Ira: 'lyrics by Arthur Francis are of the best, and seem to show that there are some lyricists who are still able to write a lyric that rhymes and also means something'. So, as it turned out, Ira had finally found his feet and had his first Broadway hit show before George.

George, though, had the ability to make friends who would push him on to the next big thing in his life. From little Maxie Rosensweig who had introduced him to serious music, to Herman and Lou Paley, early fans who had made him welcome and helped him knock off some of his rough edges, to his new friend, Jules Glaenzer, the general manager of Cartier, the exclusive Paris jeweller. At Glaenzer's glamourous Park Avenue apartment he met (and inevitably played for) producers, stars, conductors and composers. Glaenzer loved celebrities, homegrown and foreign, and his home was a regular haunt for stars such as Noel Coward, John McCormack, and Charlie Chaplin, when they were in New York.

Buddy DeSylva, encountering George at Dreyfus' office, had challenged him, more or less as a joke, to write a hit. George had immediately sat at the piano and improvised a slow, complex melody. As he finished, Buddy sang, 'Oh, do it again', meaning, play it again, but it struck them both as a great title and the beginning of a lyric which soon accompanied one of George's best tunes. He played it at Glaenzer's next party and the actress and musical star Irene Bordoni rushed through the other partygoers to reach the piano and announce breathlessly, 'I must have that damn song. It's for me!' Her husband, the producer E Ray Goetz duly bought it for her to sing in *The French Doll* and it became Gershwin's first hit of 1922.

All through the *Scandals* years George interpolated similar songs into other people's shows, including a song for Fred Astaire and his sister Adele, still trying to make their names on Broadway. In February 1922, his old friends from Remick's days, were sixth on the bill in *For Goodness Sake,* a musical produced by Alex Aarons and starring Helen Ford who, as the star, had all the best songs. But there was one, not very distinguished song, 'All to Myself', by George, and two others by the show's principal composers, Paul Lannin, ('Tra-La-La' and 'Someone', with lyrics by 'Arthur Francis') that allowed them to shine and earned them their first critical plaudit on Broadway from the New York American: 'They are the show's principal assets . . . They can speak a little, act a little and dance quarts . . .' Which was very little different from the Hollywood studio executive's subsequent 'confidential' assessment of Fred's screen test: 'Can't sing, can't act, can dance a little.'

Paul Whiteman's role as onstage music director and bandleader of the *Scandals of 1922* inevitably brought him into contact with the show's composer, George Gershwin and its lyricist, Buddy DeSylva. A trained classical violinist, Whiteman had emerged from the Wild West leading a band of nine men, one of whom, Ferde Grofé, was (with Billy Strayhorn, who worked with Duke Ellington) the pre-eminent arranger of his time. While not really a jazz orchestra, the Whiteman band in its early recordings displays a considerable jazz sensibility which owes much to the black musicians who played Harlem and New Orleans and could occasionally be found on the West Side of Chicago.

Whiteman, who loved to demonstrate his band's familiarity with the new sounds, was not averse to DeSylva's idea of including a 'jazz opera', set in Harlem, in the *Scandals,* and initially neither was George White. The Harlem renaissance was at its height – white critics were taking notice of the painting, sculpture and poetry that was emanating from the urban black communities – and mid-town 'swells' would beat a path to Harlem to listen to jazz and dance all night. 'When the sun went down Harlem was integrated,' wrote the historian, Geoffrey Perrett. Gershwin would have the opportunity to write a piece for the stage that was longer than a 3-minute revue song and to exercise the muscles he had developed in writing 'Lullaby' and several other concert works as yet unperformed.

Having committed to including it, however, White began to worry that the flow of his revue would be damaged by inserting into it a half-hour interlude in a different style. They shelved the project only to have White change his mind again about two or three weeks before the show opened. George wrote later: *DeSylva sat down with his pencil and I dug down and found a couple of suitable tunes and we began writing. After five days and nights we finished this one act vaudeville opera (which)was thought highly of by those in connection with the show, including Paul Whiteman.* Writing an opera in five days was nothing special in the Broadway of the 1920s.

George said his indigestion, or what he would for the rest of his life refer to as *composer's stomach,* dated from that opening night: *My nervousness was mainly due to* Blue Monday *(which) went very well – its only drawback for the show being its tragic ending.* He recalled one critic saying of it, 'This opera will be imitated in a hundred years.' Unfortunately another called it 'the most dismal, stupid and incredible blackface sketch that has ever been perpetrated'.

George White, having given *Blue Monday* his best shot, took it out after the New York opening because he said the audience was too depressed by the tragic ending to get in the mood for the lighter stuff that followed. *Blue Monday* can today be seen as the first flowering of what would become *Porgy and Bess,* and the beginning of George's serious dramatic interest in telling a story with harmony and tone colour as well as with melody and rhythm. It wasn't, as someone grandly said, 'The first real American opera,' but it did point the way. *Porgy and Bess* would take more than a year to compose, whereas *Blue Monday* was completed in five days. Considering that, it was a significant achievement.

The big song from that *Scandals of 1922* was 'I'll Build a Stairway to Paradise', which features what have become known as 'blue notes'. This is a musical device so identified with George Gershwin that it could be assumed that he invented it but it has existed in African-American music since African chants first hit the New World with the slave trade. Blue notes can be found in much Jewish liturgical music and in the more popular kletzmer clarinet sounds. A basic element of jazz, along with its rhythmic innovations, blue notes involve the 'bending' of notes so that the voice or instrument can more effectively 'slide' from one tone to another, adding a yearning or mournful effect to the sound. None of that music, though, was originally written down. Gershwin music specialist Rodney Greenberg characterises it thus: 'There had to be a way of categorising the most often-used blue notes and integrating them within the conventional western musical scale. Put in simple terms, composers "flattened" the third and seventh notes of the scale, effectively turning them "blue" to the ear.

(In some cases the fifth note also gets "flattened" and turns blue.) The major scale becomes the "blue-note" scale – the lifeblood, one might say, of the blues, the world of jazz, and the music of George Gershwin.'

When the *Scandals* closed Gershwin headed for Europe. It was his first trip abroad and tremendously exciting. The success of 'Swanee' in England had led to an invitation for George to score an entire revue. He was expected to write some 12 songs in less than two weeks and rehearsals started four days after he arrived. Fortunately he had packed a few 'trunk' songs in case they were needed. The result, *The Rainbow,* with sketches and linking material written by several playwrights, including Edgar Wallace, ran for 112 performances.

Two contrasting incidents characterised this first London sojourn: when George's liner docked at Southampton, the passport officer looked at his name and, properly impressed, asked, 'George Gershwin, writer of "Swanee"?' George said later, *I felt I was Kern or somebody.* Thrilled, George's time in England was coloured by the warmth of this greeting and forever afterwards he always came to London with pleasure. The second was less pleasant. An unnamed British comic in the show, whose part had been cut down further and further since George's arrival, had by opening night had enough. Coming to the footlights during his spot he harangued the audience on the evil influence of Americans on the British stage. The audience, thinking this diatribe was part of the show, began to laugh, but realised, at about the same time as did the management, that it was an impromptu display of fury. History records neither what happened to the unfortunate comedian nor his name, but it's probably safe to assume that he wasn't working in that theatre the following night.

Once *The Rainbow* was up and running, George went off with Jules Glaenzer for his first visit to Paris. Jules showed him the city, took him to a famous bordello, and gave him a spectacular party in his beautiful home on the Rue Malakoff before waving him off back to New York and the *Scandals of 1923*.

Meanwhile, Paul Whiteman was also in England for the first time, where he and his Orchestra proved to be very popular. They had played the Hippodrome, and the English interest in American popular music not as music to dance to or to sing, but just to listen to in a concert hall setting, gave him the germ of an idea. Why not exploit the new interest in jazz and popular music (which had already been harnessed by Maurice Ravel, Darius Milhaud, and other important concert music composers) by performing it in the august setting of New York's Carnegie Hall? He reasoned that if he called it *An Experiment in Modern Music* then it wouldn't have to be labelled 'jazz', which would enable him to include all kinds of American music, not just jazz. And it would not then deter potential audiences who might be frightened away by the unfamiliar.

George was himself finally heading for the concert hall. At the suggestion of his biggest fan, the arts critic Carl van Vechten, George had been engaged by the French-Canadian mezzo, Eva Gauthier, to arrange and accompany her in a group of American popular songs that would form the second half of her recital programme at New York's Aeolian Hall in the autumn of 1923. Even the first half of the programme was unconventional, containing music by Hindemith, Schoenberg and Bartok, accompanied by Max Jaffe. But when Gauthier swept onto the stage in a high-necked but backless gown for the second half, followed by a tuxedo-clad Gershwin with his gaudy song sheets, she was signalling to the audience that something almost shocking was happening. The fare was remarkable for such a setting – Irving Berlin, Jerome Kern, Walter Donaldson, and, of course, George Gershwin – and, as if to emphasise her intentions, she began with Berlin's first great hit, 'Alexander's Ragtime Band'. The set closed with 'Swanee', and the audience of New York movers and shakers, informed and sophisticated concertgoers, raised the roof. As an encore, she sang George and Buddy DeSylva's suggestive 'Do It Again', and then, at the audience's insistence, she did it again.

Deems Taylor, writing in the New York *World,* enjoyed every minute: 'The audience was as much fun to watch as the songs were to hear, for it began by being slightly patronising and ended by surrendering completely to the alluring rhythms of our own folk music.' By describing the music as 'our own', that is, American, Taylor was shrewd enough to be consciously responding to the Columbia University composition professor Daniel Gregory Mason who had earlier warned in the *New Music Review,* of the 'insidiousness of the Jewish menace to our artistic integrity'.

For Gershwin, it was a personal triumph: the first time his pianistic talents, so familiar to friends and insiders, had been made available to a wider public. He had always dreamed of playing his music to an appreciative, cultivated, concert audience. (Deems Taylor called them 'a "brilliant" house, made up of . . . people who not only cared for music but who knew something about it'.) Eva Gauthier, flushed with her own success and the boldness of her choice, booked him for a repeat performance of the same programme in Boston in January 1924. For the rest of his life, the concert hall was as much his territory as the theatre.

The great music of the past in other countries has always been built on folk-music. This is the strongest source of musical fecundity . . . I believe that it is possible for a number of distinctive styles to develop in America, all legitimately born of folk-song from different localities. Jazz, ragtime, Negro spirituals and blues, Southern mountain songs, country fiddling and cowboy songs can all be employed in the creation of American art music, and are actually used by many composers now.

GEORGE GERSHWIN

Rhapsody in Blue · 1923-1925

'In the rhythm, the melody, the humor, the grace, the rush and sweep and dynamics of his composition, he expressesd the genius of young America.'

OTTO KAHN

Following his triumph with Eva Gauthier, George headed back to the neglected Buddy DeSylva who was waiting for him to complete *The Perfect Lady*, a book musical they had started to write and which was scheduled to open in Boston at the end of 1923. *The Perfect La*dy, now retitled S*weet Little Devil,* duly opened in Boston in December and on Broadway in January. On the way to Boston, though, George had given birth to the most popular piece of American concert music ever composed.

On 4 January 1924 George and Buddy DeSylva were playing pool at the Ambassador Billiard Parlor in mid-town while Ira watched and read the newspaper. A small item in the New York *Herald Tribune* surprised him. The headline read: 'Whiteman Judges Named. Committee Will Decide, "What Is American Music".' Underneath it declared: 'George Gershwin is at work on a jazz concerto.' Paul Whiteman had arranged a concert, entitled *What is American Music?* not at Carnegie Hall which was booked solid but at the smalle but only slightly less prestigious Aeolian Hall. And the date was to be 12 February, Lincoln's Birthday, a scant five weeks away.

Ira, who was privy to almost all George's plans, had never heard of this jazz concerto. He interrupted the game. Would George like to read about himself in the newspaper? George was amazed.

Gershwin looks respectfully at Maurice Ravel seated at the piano, Eva Gauthier is standing behind the composer.

It was true that he had discussed a work with Whiteman after they had worked together on *Blue Monday*. It was true that he was interested in the concept of a concerto with himself as piano soloist. It was true that he had some ideas, a theme or two written in his notebook. But he had not begun to write it. It hadn't a centre, a concept or a shape yet, even in his head. The following morning, before leaving for Boston for the Broadway rehearsals of *Sweet Little Devil*, he telephoned Whiteman. *I can't*, he said. *There just isn't enough time. And, anyway, why didn't you talk to me first before announcing it in the paper?* Whiteman was somewhat repentant, and very persuasive. He said that he had talked too much about his vision for a concert tracing the entire history and breadth of American musical performance and now a rival bandleader, Vincent Lopez, was planning to get in first.

His plan was a concert including everything American from Zez Confrey to Kern and even such non-American fare as Edward Elgar and Rudolf Friml, which had been, or could be, given a jazz treatment. It was, he said, grandly, an 'educational' experiment and there was to be, the *Herald Tribune* reported, a jury of luminaries such as Sergey Rakhmaninov, the violinists Jascha Haifetz and Efrem Zimbalist (and his wife, the soprano, Alma Gluck) to decide, *What Is American Music?*

Whiteman was easily able to persuade Gershwin to participate, despite his other commitments. He would have hated to have been left out. On the train to Boston for the final rehearsals of *Sweet Little Devil,* he began to listen to the clackety-clack of the train as it moved along the tracks and he could suddenly hear the rhythmic scheme for his new piece. *I suddenly heard – and even saw on paper – the complete construction of the* Rhapsody *from beginning to end.*

It wouldn't, he decided, be a concerto at all but a rhapsody (its working title was *An American Rhapsody*), a form that would allow him more freedom in the writing. Those train sounds, coupled with an opening bar and a theme or two from his notebook, plus a wonderful, sensuous melody, which would form the centre of the piece, would combine to make a piece of music that was both a radical departure and a homecoming.

There are various versions of how the grand E-Major central theme of *Rhapsody in Blue* happened to end up where it is in the form that it did. In one, it came to George while improvising at a party. *All at once,* he wrote to Isaac Goldberg, his first biographer, *I heard myself playing a theme that must have been haunting me inside, seeking outlet. No sooner had it oozed out of my fingers than I knew I had it.* In another, Ira discovered it in one of George's notebooks and insisted that it was right for the *Rhapsody.* In a third, the orchestrator Ferde Grofé, disliking the 'pastoral' that George had inserted in that place, begged him to find something 'more melodic' and, on hearing the theme played by George in the key of E flat, insisted on transposing it to a key more suited to the rest of the piece. In this version, (not surprisingly, this is Grofé's version from a later newspaper interview) George initially refused, saying that it was *tripe, sentimental,* and *too cheap,* but finally succumbed to the entreaties of both Grofé and Ira.

With all that has been written about it, from the 17-note opening glissando, elided at the top as a joke by Whiteman's clarinetist, Ross Gorman, to the musicologists' note-splitting ad nauseam analysis, *Rhapsody in Blue* is a composition of sheer joy. This is not the considered classic tone poem structured by a mature sensibility, but a work full of juice and fun and sexual hi-jinks. It couldn't possibly have been written by anyone but a young man, and it is the perfect response to those who picture George Gershwin as a sad man whose life was forever blighted by a selfish mother. Listen to it, played by George himself on the early recording, or by Leonard Bernstein who

Rhapsody in Blue

recorded it twice. Listen to it played by anybody at all and then decide whether this composer was sad, or stunted, or mired in melancholy.

We know that it was written in no more than three weeks because that was the time-span between the newspaper article and the rehearsals. George wrote at white-hot speed in his workroom at his parents' apartment on 110th Street, fuelled by gallons of Russian tea, and accompanied by the sounds of Morris and his cronies' endless card games elsewhere in the apartment.

Because of the shortness of time, Whiteman's arranger Ferde Grofé came up every day, took whatever pages George had finished and orchestrated them while he was still writing. Grofé's familiarity with the strengths of individual members of the Whiteman orchestra gave the piece a richness and diversity of colour that George could never have managed on his own. This is not to say, of course, as some foolish folks have, that Ferde Grofé was the reason for the success of the piece, just that he allowed George the best possible frame for it. Perhaps most crucially, when George got cold feet and wanted to cut out the lush middle section, now the most identifiable section of the *Rhapsody*, it was Grofé who reassured him and persuaded him that it fitted.

By 29 January, when George left for his second concert with Eva Gauthier, the two-piano version was finished. By 4 February, Grofé had finished the orchestration. While he was away, Whiteman began rehearsals at the Palais Royale restaurant with the orchestra, expanded for the occasion to 23, and by the time George returned, the band was ready for him. There were then two rehearsals with George at the piano.

Whiteman often held invitation-only public rehearsals to which he invited anyone whom he thought could support the current project, usually followed by a good lunch. For both the piano rehearsals he invited critics, writers, composers such as Victor Herbert, and several fans of Gershwin's music including Henry

Osgood of *Musical America* and Carl van Vechten who had persuaded Madame Gauthier to perform her successful contemporary song set. Osgood wrote later: '. . . After hearing that second rehearsal, I never entertained a single doubt but that this young man of twenty-five had written the finest piece of serious music that had ever come out of America.'

Having played some selected tidbits to the Paleys on Saturday night, they assured him of its certain success. 'What are you going to call it?' they asked. George replied: *How about* An American Rhapsody? Everyone liked it. But Ira, who was there that evening, fresh from a Whistler exhibition at the Met in which most of the paintings had titles relating to their mood or colour – *Nocturne in Blue and Green, Harmony in Grey and Green* – suggested a name change. 'Why not call it *Rhapsody in Blue?*' It was perfect.

As the concert day approached, George was outwardly calm and apparently confident. The much more experienced Whiteman, however, lost his nerve completely. When, on the afternoon of 12 February, he looked outside the box office to see hordes of people desperately trying to get into Aeolian Hall (the manager told him later that they could have sold out 10 times over) he was so nervous that he wanted to cancel. 'Black fear simply possessed me. I paced the floor, gnawed my thumbs, and vowed I'd give $5,000 if we could stop right there and then. Now that the audience had come, perhaps I really had nothing to offer them at all.'

The Aeolian Hall 1915

Eventually Whiteman ran out of delaying tactics; someone pushed him onto the stage and the concert began. It was nearly a disaster – the ventilation system broke down and despite the cold February weather outside the hall, the tropical heat inside was very uncomfortable. Whiteman had planned a programme that was much too long and unwieldy. There were 26 items divided into 11 categories which lasted anywhere from a couple of minutes (Irving Berlin) to more than 15 (George Gershwin). It started at 2.45pm (15 minutes late) and didn't finish until 5.30. Long before that, a goodly portion of the audience was creeping surreptitiously towards the exits.

George's was the penultimate piece, before the unlikely finale of Elgar's *Pomp and Circumstance*. By that time, the auditorium was rapidly emptying. Then came *Rhapsody in Blue,* and as soon as Ross Gorman began that stunning upwardly mobile clarinet wail of an opening bar, those who were starting to leave returned to their seats. It is so difficult, 80 years on, to imagine that initial impact for those in Aeolian Hall who heard it for the first time. In form it was new, constructed of several unrelated ideas. As soon as the ear became accustomed to any one theme, it changed, shocking the listener into concentrating on the next.

Rhapsody in Blue is not programme music, not, that is, intended to conjure a particular story or image, but it is, unmistakeably, a portrait of New York. The jumpy, nervous, melodies and rhythms of the first and second themes are a perfect metaphor for the hurrying, scurrying crowds of Manhattan, the tall buildings merely a backdrop for the restless humanity teeming the narrow streets, all intent on their journeys, all *going* somewhere. And, in the *Rhapsody,* where they are heading is towards that big middle theme in E major. That rolling, roiling, romantic tune that everybody can hum is actually a destination, although we don't know that until we reach it. When the crowd is tired of its endless questing, it reaches a kind of home, not to rest there but to achieve another level of satisfaction. That middle section envelops the listener, warms him, and remains with him, even when he has to go back to the everyday world of the streets. And then again, although differently this time, because he has been changed by the experience, the *Rhapsody* speeds to its inevitable exciting conclusion.

The final chord was followed by that delicious silence that presages an explosion. Then, an audience which included socialites, critics, occasional concertgoers, regular music lovers and the great and the good of the musical world – The March King John Philip Sousa, the composers Igor Stravinsky and Victor Herbert, conductor Walter Damrosch, and violinists Jascha Heifetz and Mischa Elman – stood and roared their approval.

There was not a single member of the audience that night who didn't recognise that Gershwin had defined the time and the place in which most of them lived. Even those who didn't like the piece, or who felt that George should stick to popular music, or who thought that Jews should stay in the ghetto (and there were several of them), understood the scale of the achievement.

In those few moments – the *Rhapsody* in this original form took about 16 minutes to perform – concert music had changed; our definition of jazz had changed; New York had changed; and George Gershwin had become a star.

The critics were not quite unanimous. The majority lavished praise on the *Rhapsody:* it was '. . . greater than Stravinsky's *The Rite of Spring*', 'stunning', 'highly ingenious', and 'a really skillful piece of orchestration', showing 'genuine melodic gift', 'piquant and individual harmonic sense', 'aims that go far beyond others of his ilk'. 'Mr. Gershwin . . . may yet bring jazz out of the kitchen,' claimed one critic. 'He has expressed himself in a significant and . . . highly original manner' with 'extraordinary talent'. The two who remained unimpressed, Pitts Sanborn and Lawrence Gilman, really hated it, criticising its 'empty passage work', 'meaningless repetition', 'trite and feeble' tunes, 'sentimental and vapid' harmonies, and 'fussy and futile' counterpoint.

'Whiteman's Folly', as the concert had been dubbed (even with every seat filled it had cost Paul Whiteman at least $5,000 of his own money), succeeded, according to Gershwin's contemporary biographer David Ewan, beyond Whiteman's own wildest dreams. 'The most serious musicians and critics were discussing it with the discrimination and analytical discernment they brought to all major musical events. And it was the *Rhapsody in Blue* that . . . transformed the Whiteman experiment . . . to an artistic event of the first magnitude.'

As for George, he knew exactly what he had done and how important it was: *I heard it as a sort of musical kaleidoscope of America – of our vast melting pot, of our incomparable national pep, of our blues, our metropolitan madness.*

Somebody Loves Me

'The Rhapsody record is marvellous and it's given me more pleasure than you can imagine – I sit down to listen to it a normal healthy Englishman and by the time the second half is over, I could fling myself into the wildest excesses of emotional degeneracy.'

NOEL COWARD, IN A LETTER TO GEORGE GERSHWIN, 29 OCTOBER 1924

The success of that first concert was repeated throughout 1924 as Paul Whiteman took the *What Is American Music?* bandwagon all over the country. He was to conduct it in New York twice more in the Aeolian Hall and, finally, in April at the originally intended venue, Carnegie Hall, prior to a two-week tour with George playing the piano part culminating in a repeat of the entire concert at Aeolian Hall.

George left the tour after St Louis, ostensibly because he had other commitments, including that year's *Scandals,* and the piano part in the *Rhapsody* was taken over by Milton Rettenberg, one of only a handful of pianists, according to Ira, who could rise to its technical demands. Max Dreyfus decided to publish *Rhapsody in Blue,* much to Ira's amazement. 'I think Max is nuts,' he told George. 'Who'll buy it?'

In June 1924, the Whiteman band recorded *Rhapsody in Blue,* with George playing the piano part. This being before the invention of microphones, the recording session was acoustic, through big horns. The record became a worldwide hit, the first time a concert recording sold a million copies in what we would today call the album charts. It has been calculated that over the years the combined sales of sheet music and recordings generated a quarter of a million dollars for George alone.

Also in June, George opened the last of his consecutive *George White Scandals.* In between he somehow found time to write a whole new score for the revue, one of whose songs, with lyrics by Buddy DeSylva and Ballard MacDonald, would become one of his greatest hits and the first of his string of romantic ballads which have something to say to each generation: 'Somebody Loves Me'. Then, on 8 July, George set sail for London to work on a very English-style revue called *Primrose.* George, never happy to live alone, shared a pretty flat overlooking Devonshire Gardens with Alex Aarons and his wife Ella. George loved the 'shock of the new' and whatever he took up became fashionable: it became what Ella described as 'the latest in Georgeousness'. He loved being in London. It was full summer and he went to Wimbledon, shopped, and entertained friends ranging from the Duke of Kent to the financier Otto Kahn.

Aarons' main reason for being there was to persuade the Astaires, performing in London in *For Goodness Sake, Stop Flirting,* to return to New York to star in a new Gershwin show, tentatively entitled *Black-Eyed Susan. Primrose* opened on 11 September 1924. The backbone of the score was several new songs George had written with Ira (who was in the process of

A dazzling trio, Fred Astaire at the keyboard with George and Ira Gershwin

dropping Arthur Francis, to re-emerge as, first, Ira B Gershwin, and then plain Ira Gershwin). It was, by all accounts, a charming but forgettable show and although George hoped it would transfer to Broadway, it never did. It was, however, a considerable hit in London, running for 255 performances and the advance ticket sales by the first night of £24,000 were a record for the time. The only song still in regular currency from the show is the staccato 'Naughty Baby'. George's favourite review was one that referred to lyrics by 'his sister, Ira'. Ira was teased with that for some time.

Immediately after the opening Gershwin returned to New York to work on *Black-Eyed Susan* for Fred and Adele Astaire, taking

Guy Bolton, who had part-written the script for *Primrose,* and his co-writer Fred Thompson to construct the book. Otto Kahn, the financier, at first refused to invest in the show, saying with heavy irony that he was famous for investing only in flops but on board ship George played him the one completed song for the show and he pledged $10,000 on the spot. The song was 'The Man I Love'.

As it turned out, 'The Man I Love' was cut from the score during the pre-Broadway run in Philadelphia, but the show, retitled *Lady, Be Good!,* was now the proud possessor of one of the most innovative of all George and Ira's songs. It had started life as an 8-bar fragment in George's tunebook in London and been much admired by Alex Aarons, but when he returned to New York and played it for his brother, Ira expostulated: 'For God's sake, George, what kind of lyric do you write to a rhythm like that?'

It was a jumpy little tune with the accents in all the 'wrong' places. George loved its unexpectedness but agreed that it would be hard to turn into words. 'But,' continued Ira, picking up the odd accents, 'it's a fascinating rhythm.' It was a Eureka moment, but it still took Ira several days to settle on a rhyme scheme, a delay that typifies the difference between the collaborators. George, who was always more energetic and instinctive, drove the partnership, slowed down by his more deliberate, precise brother who wouldn't be hurried into making the wrong decision.

The brothers, Ira recalled, 'argued for days' about 'Fascinating Rhythm': where the emphasis should be placed; on which syllable and note; what rhymes should be double; and how the accents could be treated so that the song made sense musically, lyrically, and, of course, as a vehicle for Fred's and Adele's dance. George had ideas about everything – not for him the composer's lofty withdrawal from extra-musical matters. He even solved a problem Fred was having with the dance routine for 'Fascinating Rhythm' by suggesting a step that would 'travel' them off-stage to tumultuous applause. It says something about the collegial quality of their friendship that Fred had the humility to listen (and watch, as George leapt up from the piano to demonstrate) and George had the chutzpah to tell Fred Astaire what to do with his feet. But it clearly worked because, as George said, it turned into *a miraculous dance.* They toiled on, having just as good a time as they had anticipated, opening in Philadelphia on

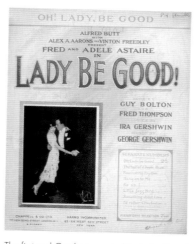

The first real Gershwin musical Lady Be Good

November 17 and continuing to hone *Lady, Be Good!* until they thought they were as ready as they'd ever be to open on Broadway. George ran back and forth between Philadelphia and New York, dealing with new orchestrations for that show, having meetings about their next show, and preparing to play the *Rhapsody* with Whiteman at a concert on 27 November.

When *Lady, Be Good!* opened on 1 December, it was a great success for everybody concerned. Finally, the Astaires were the Broadway stars they had always known they should be, and in a show that the Gershwins had written for them. All of them were well reviewed and Ira got his first 'Lyrics by Ira Gershwin are . . . excellent' notices. In a very crowded season, in which *Lady, Be Good!* was the 40th musical of the year, it was an unqualified hit. It ran for 330 Broadway performances followed by a long tour. Although it was the third (fourth, if you count *Primrose* in London) show George had in 1924, it was, in a way, the first real Gershwin musical, the one where the success of the show stood or fell on his name and the quality of his work. Everything about *Lady, Be*

Good! breathed Gershwin – the distinctive piano sound (there were two pianists in the pit), the 'jazz' rhythms, the modernity of the song structures, the muscularity of the orchestrations, and the crispness of Ira's lyrics. Audiences responded by taking the two best songs ('Fascinating Rhythm' and the title song itself) into every drawing room in New York City and beyond. All the collaborators, from the stars to the writers, were in their 20s and it showed. In the best sense this was a young show bringing much-needed vigour and innovation to a medium that was already transmuting into a true American art.

New York became a city a year after George Gershwin was born. In the decade between the two World Wars, it could be described for the first time as the centre of the world. F Scott Fitzgerald's *The Great Gatsby* was published in 1925 and its Bright Young Things were the audience for George's shows and the hosts of the parties where he played indefatigably. Fashions, always previously from France, were now created there. Design, always previously a German or Italian speciality, was now an American one. Literature, dance, drama, and now popular music, always previously English, now emanated from New York.

When 1924 ended George and Ira were both financially secure. George was actually well on the way to being rich. But they had no particular desire to set out on their own, even though Ira was engaged to Leonore (Lee) Strunsky. They bought a five-storey house on 103rd Street and Riverside Drive and, as usual, the entire Gershwin family lived together, although, when the decibel level got too high, George moved into a hotel room for a few nights. He had a rare gift for friendship, an ability to make everyone in his life feel important and valued, whether it was the Duke of Kent ('To George from George', reads the inscription on a photograph) or an earnest young music student come to interview him for the school paper.

From all accounts, the 103rd Street house was bedlam. There

was a billiard room and a ping-pong table on the ground floor, which served as a gathering point for the younger members of the family and their friends. It seems that total strangers would wander in for a game and nobody would challenge their right to be there, assuming that, if they weren't associated with the music business they must be friends of Arthur or Frances or a card-playing crony of Morris, or a mah-jong mate of Rose. The actual games took place in the living rooms on the floor above and there was a good deal of yelling from room to room about who was winning what. The third floor had bedrooms for the parents and younger Gershwins, while the fourth was Ira's and, subsequently, Ira and Lee's.

The fifth floor, however, was George's domain. Up at the top of the house he had a big sitting room lined with bookcases and full of easy chairs. He had a fireplace, his favourite Steinway and a specially built wall cabinet for his manuscripts. Here he worked,

greeted his friends, conducted his business, and gave his interviews. Here he really needed his much-vaunted power of concentration. Whatever was going on in the rest of the house, George would simply ignore it, although both he and Ira got into the habit of doing their creative writing in the small hours when the rest of their noisy clan were asleep. The photographs of them working in daylight hours were, mostly, of them revising or orchestrating, not the original songwriting. But, although

The Gershwin home on 103rd Street

Tip – Toes was a hit on all counts

at the time they moved out of the apartment on 110th Street they could easily have bought themselves a house each, plus another for their parents and younger siblings, they opted to continue to live all together as a family.

At the beginning of 1925, Ira was 29, George was just 27, and there was a lot of work to do. That year saw *Lady, Be Good!* playing happily on Broadway and then becoming a hit in London, plus the opening of three more shows on Broadway, three in London. On Broadway were the silly *Tell Me More,* which is only worth mentioning because it was originally entitled *My Fair Lady,* the pretentious operetta *Song of the Flame,* which was a success, and the charming but uneventful *Tip-Toes* which made even more money for Alex Aarons and his partner Vinton Freedley than *Lady, Be Good!* For us today, its chief claim to fame was the first appearance of a couple of Gershwin classics, 'Sweet and Low-down' and 'That Certain Feeling'.

Tip-Toes had great reviews, especially for George's music and for its star, Queenie Smith, but way down the cast list was a beautiful 19-year old with one song. Her name was Jeanette MacDonald and within the year she was in Hollywood becoming one of its biggest ever musical stars. Ira, too, was thrilled with his work on *Tip-Toes,* especially when he received a gracious fan letter from Lorenz Hart, Richard Rodgers' brilliant lyricist: 'Such delicacies as your jingles prove that songs can be both popular and intelligent . . . I have heard none so good in many a day.'

Concerto in F · 1925 - 1928

'George at the piano was George happy'   ROUBEN MAMOULIAN

When George left New York in May 1925 for two happy productive months in Europe, he took with him *four or five books on musical structure to find out what the concerto form really was,* because the conductor Walter Damrosch and Harry Harkness Flagler, President of the New York Symphony Society, had commissioned one from him. Although George was a star, always in the newspapers – the society columns as well as the arts pages – and his songs were everywhere, he was thrilled by this sign of trust from the classical music establishment, which he longed to join. He admired Flagler's guts, especially as the Society seldom solicited work from contemporary composers, least of all Americans. *It showed great confidence on his part as I had never written anything for symphony before.* (Though there were later orchestral versions, George originally scored *Rhapsody in Blue* for a jazz band.)

By the time he returned home in late June, Gershwin had already sketched some ideas for the concerto, which would premiere in December with George as soloist. Through the heat of a New York summer he marshalled these ideas into a coherent whole. He was determined to do it all himself and, as always, he was conscious of his lack of formal musical education. He planned two months for the actual composing and one month for orchestration – his own, not Ferde Grofé's. At the same time, he was finishing *Tip-Toes* and working on the operetta, *Song of the Flame.*

The house at 103rd Street became unendurably noisy and

crowded, so George reverted to his habit of moving into a hotel to work. But his friends continued to visit him at the hotel until he was rescued by his friend Ernest Hutcheson, the Australian Dean of Music at the Juilliard School, who offered him a cottage in Chattauqua, an upstate New York musical colony for Juilliard students where Hutcheson taught master classes in a peaceful, idyllic setting.

As busy as he was, it is hard to believe that George had time to keep up with his friends or to see girlfriends. He wrote regularly to Pauline Heifetz, Jascha Heifetz's sister, who at one time hoped he would propose to her. More intriguingly, he was also seeing one Mollie Charleston, who, under her stage name of Margaret Manners, appeared in a number of Broadway shows. There is a persistent rumour, never substantiated that Mollie, who was married at the time, gave birth to George's son in May 1926. But had this been true, the child would have been conceived the previous August, while George was at Chattauqua, and had Mollie been writing him, or he Mollie, during that time, it is unlikely the affair would not have come to light, given the nature of the communal living arrangements there.

The rumour persists because Alan Schneider (the name on the boy's birth certificate) bears a superficial physical resemblance to George and has insisted throughout his life that he was told by his parents, Mollie's sister Fanny and her husband Ben, that Gershwin was his father. As far as I have been able to determine, there is no foundation whatsoever for this claim, which is sad, as it would have been lovely to have even a fraction of George Gershwin's talent passed on to a son.

According to George's contract with the orchestra, the title of the new work was *New York Concerto*. For a fee of $500, he promised to appear as soloist in seven performances including at the official premiere on 3 December in New York. Late in the summer, however, as the working title disappeared and *Concerto in F* began to emerge, George played his work in progress for his friends at parties as he always did. Consequently, many of the New York cognoscenti had already heard it, or parts of it, long before the leaves changed colour. Unlike most composers, George was happy to present his work as it progressed.

Two weeks before the Carnegie Hall premiere, George gathered about 50 professional musicians at the Globe Theatre for a test run of the full work with William Daly conducting. George invited Ernest Hutcheson, whose opinion on any piano-related matters he respected, and of course the conductor, Walter Damrosch. These three all suggested some changes but it is certainly not true, as has been suggested, that Daly orchestrated *Concerto in F,* or that Damrosch insisted on changes to the piano solos that in any way unbalance the work. Contemporary musical thought indicated that the most Damrosch did was to 'thicken' the orchestral sound with a little more instrumentation than was in the original draft.

The *Concerto in F* is written in traditional form – a fast movement, a slow one, and then a faster finale. The first movement takes its character from a popular dance – the Charleston – although it's the most traditional of the three movements. The entire piece puts a full symphony orchestra through its paces far more rigorously than does *Rhapsody in Blue* and it includes complex rhythms and unusual harmonies, which gave the symphony players unaccustomed difficulties. The slow middle movement is more bluesy and nocturnal, with quirky, even delicate patterns in the solo piano passages. The finale starts with a rewrite of one of his 'trunk' themes, a piano Prelude which was to have been the first of 24, one of his few classical projects to have been abandoned. (It is odd, as the concert pianist and Gershwin specialist, Jeffrey Siegel, points out, that a composer who thought directly into the piano and who used the instrument as his confidant, wrote so little solo piano music.)

This third movement is described by George as *an orgy of rhythm,* which pulls the entire composition together and utilizes melodies and rhythms from both the preceding movements. Gershwin draws here on material from his many influences – you can hear Charleston, ragtime syncopation, and, of course, blues. But although *Concerto in F,* like all his work, contains many jazz elements (syncopation, standard tunes, bluesy harmonies), this is, by any measure, a classical, concert-hall-bound composition.

The capacity audience at the official premiere on the afternoon of 3 December 1925 included Sergei Rakhmaninov, Jascha Heifetz, and many other musical luminaries. Because of his tryouts with Daly earlier, and the orchestral reading at the Globe, George already knew the *Concerto in F* worked. What he didn't know was how it would be received by the music critics or by the notoriously fickle musical public. While he had a healthy (and earned) respect for his own pianistic skills, he was understandably apprehensive about fronting New York's premiere symphony orchestra for a famous and exacting Maestro.

In the event, he need not have worried. The audience were noisily enthusiastic, the celebratory parties sparkled, the champagne flowed and backstage the atmosphere was electric. The classical stars – Rakhmaninov, Heifetz, Hoffman – *complimented me on my piano execution,* exulted George, adding that even celebrated musicians *paid me compliments on my efforts as a composer.* There were not one, but two parties that day, one in the afternoon, where Jules Glaenzer gave George a gold cigarette case inscribed 'To George Gershwin and his First Concerto' and signed by more than two dozen of his musical and theatrical friends, another in the evening at the home of Walter Damrosch and his wife. Lester Donahue was at the Damrosch party. 'He was very happy that night,' Donahue recalled of George, 'pleased with the reception of his concerto and also over his first appearance as pianist with Damrosch at Carnegie Hall.'

The next day the reviewers, as usual, split between those who didn't care for the *Concerto*, calling it 'trite' and 'crude', and those who recognised George's extraordinary ability to embody the spirit of his time and place. Samuel Chotzinoff in the (New York) *World* called George's *Concerto* a work of 'genius'. 'He is the present, with all its audacity, impertinence, its feverish delight in its motions, its lapses into rhythmic exotic melancholy.' Even Olin Downes in the *Times*, while not completely convinced

'There were passages vivid and humorous - a sort of chattering of Broadway chorus girls drinking mint julep at Child's. There were slow secretive melodies that had in them something of the mystery of vast forests. The tunes clashed and fought, degenerated, were made clean again, joined together, and scampered madly over the keyboard in a final rush which was as breathless as the thundering herd over the prairies of the West.'

musically, had to admit the enthusiastic and instant success of the work with the audience: 'At the end of the performance the popularity of the composer was attested in long and vehement applause, so that Mr. Gershwin was kept bowing for some minutes from the stage.'

In the first two weeks of December 1925, in between the first public performances of *Concerto in F* – in New York, Washington DC, Baltimore and Philadelphia – George was not exactly idle. His musical, *Tip-Toes,* again for Aarons and Freedley, which he was writing concurrently with the *Concerto,* was trying out in Newark, New Jersey, while his operetta with Oscar Hammerstein II, *Song of the Flame,* was about to open in Wilmington, Delaware.

While in Philadelphia for a performance of the *Concerto,* George received a telegram from Pauline Heifetz in what was probably a last-ditch effort to encourage him to propose to her. Their mutual friend, the pianist and critic Samuel Chotzinoff, had asked her to marry him, she cabled. It had the opposite effect from what she intended. George, never in love with her, but genuinely wanting her to be happy, cabled back, *Wonderful.* Pauline married 'Chotzie' and from all accounts it was a highly successful union, although George later told his sister Frankie that at the time he had been too busy to pay attention, from which she inferred that he might have made a different response had he had the time to think about it.

'Fascinatin' Rhythm'

'There goes George Gershwin with the future Mrs Kay Swift'

OSCAR LEVANT

The success of *Concerto in F* reopened the argument, first heard at the time of the *Rhapsody in Blue,* about whether George should now abandon Broadway to concentrate on composing for the concert hall and the opera house. Walter Damrosch admitted trying to persuade Gershwin that he was too good for the light theatre: 'I felt he had it in him to develop on more serious lines than Broadway shows demanded or even permitted. But the lighter forms, in which he had become a master, proved too strong.' He later said: 'Perhaps I was wrong and his own instinct guided him towards what he felt most able to do.'

With the benefit of nearly a century of musical history since this debate, it is easy now to dismiss this apparent conflict between 'serious' and 'light' music as inconsequential, but that would be to underestimate the state of turmoil in the arts in America at the start of the The Jazz Age.

Art Deco, as it was referred to in Europe, was influencing clothes, architecture, painting – every aspect of people's lives. World War One, quite apart from murdering an entire generation of young men, changed the habits of every family in the Western world. Men were coming home from the war to women who were no longer biddable. They wanted to retain the rights and responsibilities they had been forced to take on while the men were away and they wanted a good time as a reward for keeping the home fires burning, as Ivor Novello's hit song had it. The men too no longer 'knew their place'. They had spent four years of unimaginable hell in the muddy trenches of France and they knew their officers, what remained of them, were no better than they were. These returning men and new women were ready to kick up their heels and start an entirely new kind of society, one in which hedonism and idealism lived side by side. Old Europe was exhausted; new ideas would have to come from somewhere else. That somewhere else was an ocean away.

America, spared the war on its own soil, now stepped forward to lead with a lighter step. George was just too young to have gone to war but he was keenly aware that, had it gone on longer, there was every chance he, as a young man from an immigrant family, would not have had the 'pull' to get himself excluded from the military. Ira, in fact, was drafted in 1918. At Grand Central Station he boarded a train with other teenagers bound for induction boot camp but it never left the station. Finally, after hours of waiting, they were told to 'go home and wait for the call'. It never came. The Armistice had been signed.

From Europe came refugees – musicians, painters, directors and designers – to make a new life in America, and especially New York. These Europeans were hungry to be Americans, to transform themselves from depressed and malnourished idealists, often performing in basements for a meal, into a community of artists who were well paid and appreciated. Orchestras and chamber music societies proliferated, all over the United States. Theatres were built in places where before there hadn't even been places. Art galleries and museums suddenly began to acquire contemporary works where there had been only Old Masters. In turn, these new Americans influenced the places they had left. A new freedom now permeated the coffeehouses and cabarets of

Berlin, Paris, and London, as well as New York. In all these cities now, ideas were exchanged, songs were written, and scandals were hatched. Hair was bobbed; skirts grew ever shorter. The coming of labour-saving devices and the virtual disappearance of domestic servants into better paying jobs changed the home lives of millions.

The initial suspicion and discrimination each wave of immigrants experienced – 'No Dogs or Irish' – gave way to an appreciation of what they had to offer. Just as the more physical Irish excelled in sports and became the backbone of the Fire and Police departments, and the rural Scandinavians colonised the mid-West farmlands, so the Jews came to the cities and exploited their artistic, mercantile and academic talents. They sewed, they taught, they sold and they bought, and with the other immigrants they formed the mass of exploding energy that was New York.

Early in 1925, at a party for Jascha Heifetz, George had met the woman who came closer than any other to a partner for life. Her name at the time was Kay Swift Warburg, wife of the banker, James Paul Warburg, mother of three, a year older than George and the giver of sparkling parties, which attracted the cream of New York artistic and intellectual society. Kay was beautiful and sexually alluring with gorgeous clothes and the manners to match. But she was more than a rich woman who liked celebrities: she was a trained musician, daughter of a music critic, granddaughter of a composer, and an accomplished pianist. She understood all the academic disciplines of music – theory, counterpoint, orchestration – which George occasionally felt lacking in his own auto-didact's education. George and Kay could perhaps have been two halves of the same whole. It never happened (George's choice, not Kay's) but their relationship lasted, albeit on a non-exclusive basis, for the rest of George's life.

It may be just a coincidence that George and Ira's next major musical would be entitled *Oh, Kay!* Edward Jablonski says that the title came from the writers of the book and lyrics, Guy Bolton and P G Wodehouse, not from George. However, by the time they started work on it, Kay Swift was an integral part of George's life and it was typical of him to include the name of his current woman in a song or show title. From his earliest invitations to ritzy parties he had inserted the name of whichever showgirl happened to be sitting next to him on the piano bench into the lyrics of a song. Kay, of course, became a good deal more important to him than the endless stream of pretty girls who seemed, like stray cats, to follow him home from parties, but the same treatment was part of his regular 'line' with ladies. If it ain't broke, he reasoned, don't fix it.

At the end of another phenomenal year, 1925, *Tip-Toes* opened at the Liberty, Paul Whiteman revived Gershwin's *Blue Monday,* the one-act opera

'When I met him nothing let me down. He played wonderfully and he was exactly like his music in person . . . Oh, it was so stimulating. I've seen very old people and kids, and people who were very stiffo about popular music or playing music for shows, and they rushed to the piano and hung over it . . . they were so stimulated that some of them were even starting to do a dance. People became unselfconscious; that was the great thing he did for people – one of the great things.'

KAY SWIFT

from the *Scandals,* at Carnegie Hall and renamed it *135th Street.* On 30 December, *Song of the Flame* arrived in New York at the 44th Street Theatre. As usual, not pausing for breath, George showed no signs of tiring.

Someone to Watch Over Me

'Please be careful what you write in future or I won't be answerable for the consequences.'   NOEL COWARD

After all this activity, settling the entire family (and all their friends) into the house on 103rd Street and his never-ending search for a new teacher, provided a welcome respite in the beginning of 1926. George began to paint, a refuge more than a hobby, which he took to with all the fervour a party animal can bring to a quiet, reflective occupation. For the rest of his life painting would be his refuge from an over-full schedule, an over-active mind, and a preoccupation with the company of others. He was good and he got better. His best works, including a couple of now-famous self-portraits, tell us as much about his sense of humour as about how he saw himself.

Mindful, as always, of how much he had to learn, he began to look at the paintings of others more carefully and, with uncanny instinct, he started a small collection. *My cousin, the artist,* Henry Botkin (known in the family as Harry) advised him. When Harry settled in Paris in the mid-20s he was charged with looking for works that might appeal to George's increasingly refined taste. When he found something he thought his cousin might like, he would have the work photographed and George would bid for the picture by cable or mail. In this fashion he acquired Picasso, Modigliani, Utrillo, Gauguin, and his favourite, Rouault. (*If only I could put Rouault into music,* he once said.) All were then considered to be somewhat modern and daring but subsequently proved to be not only masters of the century but very good investments. There is no record that he was aware of being shrewd in his purchases; he loved good painting and paid whatever it cost, even over the odds.

The partygoing continued, but George now began to give his own parties, and Sunday evenings became synonymous with the gatherings at 103rd Street. All the family and friends were welcome and George's sister Frances, who was then about 20, remembered sitting in the corner watching the Great and the Good gathered around the piano. Little by little, she too drew closer until her clear soprano voice, and pretty dancing, made her interpretations of George's songs popular not only at her own house but also in those of their friends. George was a little old-fashioned when it came to the notion of his own sister going on the stage but he paid for her dance lessons and in company encouraged her to shine.

That house was a permanent party, where strangers who fancied a game of billiards on the ground-floor table wandered in and mixed with the family and their friends, nobody being quite sure who had invited whom, but everyone made welcome. Rose was still cooking for whoever showed up and Pop, who had retired by this time, played cards or introduced himself to the children's friends with endless wisecracks and jokes. Then there were the dogs – George's wire-haired terrier, Tony, was always underfoot and Pop had a succession of more or less well-behaved mutts. The overall effect was, from all accounts, mayhem.

In March, George was going to London for the opening of his Broadway hit *Lady, Be Good!* There were a few adjustments to be made, a modicum of musical engineering, a little light tinkering with the language for the lyrics, but essentially the show that opened at the Empire Theatre in the West End was the one the Liberty Theatre in New York had seen on its opening night.

George had a wonderful time. He was welcomed everywhere and he was again the darling of high society. The previous year Lady Mountbatten had brought back a copy of the sheet music of 'The

Man I Love' before it was dropped from the New York production of *Lady, Be Good!* and it was now played by the top celebrity orchestras in London nightclubs. Even the Prince of Wales competed for his attention. The few days George was able to spend in Paris, staying with his old friend Mabel Schirmer, proved to be another round of parties, musicales and glamorous nights.

Two days before *Lady, Be Good!* was to open in the West End George attended Paul Whiteman's London debut with his Concert Orchestra at which George's *Rhapsody in Blue* was to be the centerpiece. Recently, Whiteman had started believing his own publicity, always a mistake, and enjoying his self-bestowed title of 'The King of Jazz'. This, he seemed to think, allowed him to change, syncopate, bend, and otherwise pull out of shape the works of whatever composer he was conducting. This he proceeded to do with George's *Rhapsody,* a mistake that caused a rift

William Freedley, the producer, explained that the opening scene of *Lady, Be Good!* had to be extended: 'Like George Gershwin, the Astaires have a large society following, and as these people come to theatre even later than they do in New York, we felt it would be better to hold off the entrance of our stars until the house was in.' In other words, the aristos and socialites who were both friends and fans of Fred and Adele arrived at the theatre after cocktails or dinner, whenever they felt like it, and the show was adjusted accordingly.

between the two innovators that would never really heal.

Lady, Be Good! opened at the Empire, Leicester Square on Wednesday 13 April 1926 in the most glittering premiere of the season. The Square was completely jammed with the cars of the haute monde and Fred and Adele Astaire needed a police escort even to get near the Stage Door. Robert Schirmer reported that 'every entrance and exit was greeted by literal cheering such as I have only heard previously at football and baseball games. It was a triumph'. The audience refused to leave and insisted on curtain speech after curtain speech. The guest list for the party afterwards at the Embassy Club, London's most fashionable nightclub, was a society and theatrical *Who's Who* and George stayed until eight in the morning, gleefully playing the score over and over for anyone who asked for it.

Lady, Be Good! ran in London, as in New York, for nine months (until the Empire shut down to become the cinema it is today) and then went on the road on a British tour for three months more. The Astaires had done two years for George in the show they had promised each other way back when George was at Remick's ('I wish one day I could write a show and you could be in it') and it was time for them all to go home to New York and work on their next musical. They were now three of the biggest stars on either side of the Atlantic.

The fourth great musical star in London at the time was Gertrude Lawrence ('Call me Gertie, everyone does') who was Noel Coward's great friend and partner and who, when not starring in a show

Gershwin adored his close friend Mabel Schirmer

Noel had written for her, headlined the revues of André Charlot on both sides of the Atlantic. Both Aarons and Freedley and Ziegfeld had offered her their next Broadway shows. But when she heard that George Gershwin was on board to write the songs for the Aarons/Freedley show, then tentatively called *Mayfair,* she signed on and became the first Englishwoman to originate a starring role in a Broadway show.

Noël Coward and Gertrude Lawrence, she starred in Oh, Kay! on both sides of the Atlantic

Ira was to write the lyrics and, in his usual methodical way, he began work almost as soon as George got off the boat from London. George, of course, instantly fell back into his usual round of parties only now he had Kay Swift Warburg on his arm. *Mayfair,* which had already been renamed *Cheerio,* became *Oh, Kay!,* long before opening night.

Halfway through the writing of the score Ira had to have an emergency appendectomy. As was usual in those pre-antibiotic times, he was in hospital for six weeks. In the interim, Howard Dietz (who, with his partner Arthur Schwartz, would go on to write such classic songs as 'Dancing in the Dark') volunteered to step in and help with the lyrics in Ira's absence.

It was not a happy experience for any of the team. Contrary to their usual practice of working with the same colleagues over and over in a close circle of professional and personal friends, neither Gershwin ever worked with Dietz again. Dietz clearly felt exploited by George and Ira – 'George, realising that any sum paid me would have to come out of Ira's royalties, paid me next to nothing,' he wrote bitterly – while Ira felt Dietz claimed too much credit for what he did. What is indisputable is that during Ira's absence Dietz came up with one of the most famous of all song titles – 'Someone To Watch Over Me' – and, when Ira returned, he kept the title but threw out Dietz's lyrics.

Guy Bolton and P G Wodehouse delivered the book late, by which time the production schedule was nearly upon them, and a grand old muddle it is too. Trying for topicality, referring to Prohibition and all that, it was about rum-smuggling off the coast of Long Island and involved a Duke whose sister, played by Gertie, disguises herself as a maid. Unplayable today, it was a gentle, whimsical frame on which to hang at least one of the greatest songs ever written for the musical theatre.

During the out-of-town previews for *Oh, Kay!* George had given Gertie Lawrence a little rag doll, which he suggested she use on-stage. Instead of standing in the middle of the stage in a spotlight singing the show's main ballad to the audience – as was customary – Gertie sang the whole of 'Someone To Watch Over Me' to the rag doll and brought the house down every night.

The Gershwins and their producers continued to tinker with the show throughout the out-of-town run. Eight songs were discarded and replaced, not because they were bad songs ('The Man I Love', one of George's greatest compositions, didn't make the cut again) but because they didn't move the show forward or perhaps didn't tell the story that needed to be told at that point in the score. But by the time *Oh, Kay!* opened on Broadway on 8 November 1926 at the Imperial Theatre it was as polished as the brass railings in the balcony. It ran for 256 performances (a full eight months, nothing by comparison with a *Cats* or *Phantom*, but a major hit for its time) and on opening night Brooks Atkinson, the *New York Times* critic, called it 'intensely delightful'.

In December 1926, George went back to the concert stage, this time with the celebrated contralto Marguerite d'Alvarez who had heard his concerts with Eva Gauthier and was anxious to try her own voice out on a set of Gershwin songs. George was not only her accompanist (or associate artiste, as today's jargon would have it), he also agreed to open the concert with a solo piano version of the *Rhapsody.* After the interval, George introduced a world premiere, his *Five Preludes* for the piano. These *Preludes,* originally conceived as part of *The Melting Pot,* a planned set of 24 preludes that he had begun in 1924, were well received and nobody seemed to notice that one of them formed the first theme for the last movement of the *Concerto in F.* Rule Number One: never waste anything, particularly not good musical ideas.

The concert was a great success as it was when they repeated it two weeks later in Buffalo and the following month in Boston. For these follow-up engagements George played a two-piano *Rhapsody* with Isadore Gorn at the other keyboard in Buffalo and Edward Hart at the other piano in Boston. Of the five *Preludes* George played that first night at the Hotel Roosevelt, three have entered the standard repertoire; the other two, as far as I know, have never been performed since in their original form. These two were clearly taken from an early tunebook in which George wrote down sketches for what he called 'novelettes', one he called *Novelette in Fourths,* the other is simply marked, *Rubato.* George later turned these two little *Preludes* into a violin and piano piece for his friend, Samuel Dushkin, known as *Short Story.*

It is said by serious pianists desperate to get their hands on it, that George Gershwin played another, sixth *Prelude*, at the Boston concert although no complete manuscript in George's hand has ever surfaced. Edward Jablonski believes that, remarkably, Gershwin simply improvised the sixth *Prelude* that night from a previously composed melody, a fragment from an old Tune Book dated January 1924, marked 'Sleepless Night'. After George's death, Kay notated 'Sleepless Night' from memory and there was a plan for Ira to write a lyric for it but the song was never completed.

Funny Face

'I don't know whether George Gershwin was born into this world to write rhythms for Fred Astaire's feet or whether Fred Astaire was born into this world to show how the Gershwin music should really be danced.'
ALEXANDER WOOLCOTT

In the spring of 1927, when George returned from a sporty holiday – skiing in Canada, golfing in Florida and deep-sea fishing – he was refreshed and ready to get back to composing, but before that, there was one more chore to complete. Although *Rhapsody in Blue* had been recorded just after its premiere, in June 1924, microphones had now been invented and Whiteman wanted to do it again using state of the art equipment. The Victor Talking Machine Company was keen to show what their new machines could do so on 21 April 1927, Paul Whiteman's Orchestra and George Gershwin met in the Liederkranz Hall in New York to make a second and this time 'electrical' recording of the *Rhapsody in Blue*.

Gershwin and Paul Whiteman

As George had feared from hearing his old friend in London, Whiteman's view of himself as 'King of Jazz' had affected his musical judgment. To be fair, by a natural process of attrition, the orchestra had changed personnel in the intervening years. Most crucially, the clarinetist Ross Gorman, whose opening glissando had done so much to define the sound of *Rhapsody in Blue,* is missing from the second recording.

Gershwin and Whiteman quarrelled at the beginning of the session about Whiteman's belief that speeding up certain passages made them jazzier. It was clear to George that the more Whiteman conducted the *Rhapsody,* the more idiosyncratic and odd his interpretation became and George's temper frayed as the tempo increased. The row culminated in the excitable Whiteman storming out of the Hall. When he had calmed down he returned, but found Nat Shilkret, the Victor Company's Director of Light Music, had taken over the podium. Out Whiteman stamped again, this time for good, and although the credit on the released recording remains with him, it was Shilkret who actually conducted.

Listening to the two recordings, less than three years apart, is fascinating. While the first version has all the hallmarks of its time – the over-literal emphasis, the occasional sloppiness of both technique and memory, the fuzziness of acoustical sound – the effect is of being present at an altogether extraordinary musical revolution and of being in the presence of genius. The second, while much tidier, note-perfect, and more technically competent, has an irritable George Gershwin, less freedom in both solo and ensemble playing, and tempos which are over-strict.

Eventually, George Gershwin and Paul Whiteman patched up their quarrel but their differences remained. Several years later, in 1930, George agreed to promote the bio-pic about Whiteman, inevitably entitled *King of Jazz,* and even appeared with him on-stage at its premiere, where they played *Rhapsody in Blue* together for the last time. Shortly after the Wall Street Crash, George was paid a whopping $50,000 for the use of the *Rhapsody* in the movie.

Recording over, George and Ira thought they had better apply themselves to their new musical. Life at 103rd Street was as busy as ever and they needed somewhere to write where there was space and peace. Ira had married Lee in September 1926 and the three of them, with Kay Swift often joining them, had rented a farm in Ossining, NY, only 30 miles from Manhattan, but far enough away to be rural and isolated. George bought his first car, a second-hand Mercedes and they all learned to drive. Predictably, George loved driving and spent days, alone and with friends, tooling round the lovely countryside, while Ira never drove again, leaving Lee to do the honours, even after they moved to California. They worked at night and enjoyed the house and the surrounding gentle hills during the day. They planned to remain there from April through September 1927, but life just got so demanding that they finally gave up in July and moved back to the sweltering inferno of a Manhattan summer.

In the meantime, though, George and Ira wrote most of the score for one of their favourite shows. *Strike Up the Band* was way ahead of its time. It was a true book musical, not a fluffy construct like *Oh, Kay!* on which the songs, dances, star vehicles and chorus numbers could be conveniently draped, but a script of substance written by George S Kaufman, the noted writer and humourist. *Strike Up the Band* had a plot, so the songs needed to push the story along. Even more ambitiously, the songs had to carry Kaufman's virulently anti-war message.

Today, it is understood that songs in musicals are deliberately integrated into the action and, more often than not, *are* the action. Nobody would expect a Sondheim musical to be a string of unrelated songs that go to the top of the Hit Parade. But in 1927 that is exactly what audiences expected of George Gershwin. They were accustomed to stand-alone hits, and, with the single exception of the title march, not one song from the original score of *Strike Up the Band* was extricable from its dramatic context within the show.

George and Ira and their producer, Edgar Selwyn, really believed in this show, politically and theatrically. A satire on war profiteers, corruption and international vanity, Kaufman had written a literate script that, with their songs, was, they thought, an American operetta in the style of Gilbert and Sullivan.

Strike Up the Band opened to great reviews in Long Branch, New Jersey on 29 August but it soon became clear that something was very wrong. Audiences didn't understand this dark, funny satire, didn't care for the songs (although Selwyn had insisted on including the hit much-excised 'The Man I Love'), and didn't see why they couldn't have a light, conventional, no-brainer like all the others. It could be argued now, with history on our side, that 1927 was on the one hand, too far from World War One for the audience still to care and on the other, too far from World War Two when they would start caring again. And who were Gilbert and Sullivan, anyway?

After two weeks of diminishing box-office receipts Edgar Selwyn closed the show, deciding that it would be foolish to go to Broadway with a musical satire that hadn't found its feet yet. But he didn't lose faith in it. He knew that he had the makings of an important musical and, with the benefit of hindsight, we can see exactly where it fit – alongside *Show Boat,* which immediately followed it and which dealt with racism and hypocrisy, and *Carousel,* some 20 years later, a book musical about death and crime. It would be back and then, Selwyn knew, it would be a hit.

In the meantime, George and Ira had commitments to Aarons and Freedley who needed a show to follow *Lady, Be Good!* for the

Gertrude Lawrence performing with the London cast of Oh, Kay!

Astaires, and another for Gertrude Lawrence, then just finishing her long London run in *Oh, Kay!*

The book for the new project for the Astaires was to be written by the brilliant New Yorker humourist, Robert Benchley, and the experienced book-writer Fred Thompson who had written *Lady, Be Good!* with Guy Bolton, and *Tip-Toes.* Unfortunately, the script they turned in, *Smarty,* was a shambles even by the generous standards of the late 20s. It was one thing for the audience to resent a show like *Strike Up the Band,* which made them think too much, but *Smarty* was asking them to check whatever brains they had at the door with their coats.

Smarty opened on 11 October, less than a month after *Strike*

Up the Band had closed ignominiously and for a while it looked as though *Smarty* would follow the same path. Ira told Jablonski: 'Everyone concerned with the show worked day and night, recasting, rewriting, rehearsing, recriminating – of rejoicing was there none.' There had been so many changes to his script that Robert Benchley asked to have his credit removed and that he not receive any royalties. George and Ira wrote 24 songs for this show, now retitled *Funny Face,* at least twice as many as would be needed, but the requirements of the show changed night by night and perfectly lovely George/Ira concoctions got lost in the search for the perfect song for the right place. Relationships were strained to breaking point, even those between the Gershwins and their longtime friends and producers, Alex Aarons and Vinton Freedley, who at one point were so fed up with the Gershwins' changes that they insisted that George share the cost of copying the new orchestrations.

The producers had built a new Broadway theatre, the Alvin, on the profits from their Gershwin association and had had it designed expressly with big musicals in mind. At this stage they were seriously worried that this particular vehicle would open their new space with a fizzle rather than a dazzle. At the friendship's lowest point, Ira Gershwin wrote the last song to be inserted into *Funny Face,* a scabrous little ditty about the superficiality of friendship, 'The Babbitt and the Bromide', which some years later achieved fame in *That's Entertainment* as the vehicle for the only ever joint film appearance of Fred Astaire and Gene Kelly.

In the event, Aarons and Freedley need not have worried. After six exhausting weeks on the road, *Funny Face* opened at the Alvin on 22 November 1927. The critics were scathing about the script ('flat', 'scrambled', 'perishable') but they were mad about the songs, the stars, the sets and the theatre itself.

They reserved their most extravagant praise for the Astaires and the Gershwins. George Jean Nathan said, 'If there are better dancers anywhere I must have been laid up with old war wounds when they displayed themselves.' *Funny Face* ran at the Alvin for 244 performances and, inevitably, repeated its success the following year in London's West End.

While holed up in Philadelphia suffering the birth pangs of *Funny Face,* George and Ira had more or less forgotten that they had made a commitment to Ziegfeld for a new musical to star the young phenomenon, Marilyn Miller. By the time *Funny Face* had been spawned, though, their new musical *Rosalie* was already in rehearsal and the Gershwins had to work uncomfortably fast. Ziegfeld's original plan was that George would share the music with operetta king, Sigmond Romberg, and that Ira would write the lyrics with P G Wodehouse but there wasn't time for extensive collaboration.

Ira and 'Plum' Wodehouse did write some lyrics together but, mainly, Romberg's songs and the Gershwins' were separate entities. George and Ira dug deep into the 'trunk' and the tunebooks and came up with, of course, 'The Man I Love', which had still not made it to Broadway, as well as five others which were serviceable enough, while Romberg's operetta arias reflected the romantic and sentimental story about a visiting princess who falls in love with a US Army officer, loosely based on the recent visit to America of Queen Marie of Rumania.

This muddle shouldn't have worked, but it did, even without 'The Man I Love' which was, inevitably, cut on the road. The critics liked it; Ziegfeld was ecstatic. The Gershwins were tired. So in March 1928 they scooped up Lee and their sister, Frankie, and set sail for Europe. For the other three it was to be their first trip across the Atlantic. For George, it was to be his last.

'Why should you be a second-rate Ravel when you can be a first-rate Gershwin?'
MAURICE RAVEL

George's thank you to the Schirmers for their Paris hospitality the previous year had been a professionally taken photograph of himself signed with a couple of musical quotes. The first was clearly the main theme from the *Rhapsody* but the other was unfamiliar, three bars marked 'An American in Paris'.

With *Funny Face* and *Rosalie* running on Broadway and *Oh, Kay!* in the West End, George was keen to return to the concert hall. The popular notion that after *Funny Face* George went off to Paris and, while there, just happened to write *An American in Paris* is a romantic one but, unfortunately, not true. He had, in fact, written both a solo-piano version and a 70-page two-piano reduction of the work before he ever left New York.

On the way to Paris the three Gershwins took a whistle-stop few days in London to see Gertie Lawrence close *Oh, Kay!* She took George shopping in Jermyn Street and Savile Row for clothes and made a tearful curtain speech, marking the end of the highly successful West End run of *Oh, Kay!*

Nadia Boulanger

George was, as usual, on his search for a teacher when he arrived in Paris. He had previously approached Ravel, already a fan, and Prokofiev, who wasn't. Ravel turned him down because, as he told Eva Gauthier, 'it would probably cause him to write bad Ravel'. Prokofiev wasn't interested. When George talked to Stravinsky the older composer asked him how much he had earned from his music in the preceding year. Startled, George did a quick calculation

First the Bach Passacaglia, orchestrated by Stokowski. Then, a symphony by Mozart or Beethoven, preferably the latter's Fifth or Seventh. I'd want Stravinsky on the program too, represented by either his 'Petrouchka' or 'Le Sacre du Printemps'. And I'd wind up the concert with Richard Strauss' 'Till Eulenspiegel'. As alternate pieces I'd like to hear Debussy's 'L'après-midi d'un faune' or one of Bach's Brandenburg Concertos.

GEORGE GERSHWIN DESCRIBES HIS

IDEAL CONCERT

and told him, somewhere over $100,000. 'Well, my young friend,' Stravinsky retorted, impressed, 'then perhaps I ought to study with you.'

Ravel had given him an introduction to Nadia Boulanger's Paris studio. Although still in her 20s, Mademoiselle, as she was invariably known, even to her intimates, was the teacher of almost all the major American composers of the early 20th century, most notably of Aaron Copland. Boulanger also rejected George as a student and for nearly the same reasons as Ravel. Boulanger felt that there was little she could teach him. Further, she told him that her strictly academic approach (widely attested to by Copland and others) could inhibit his natural gifts. He took the refusal in good part, knowing that it was, in its way, a compliment. In fact, Mademoiselle and George became good friends on that visit to her studio, a relationship which continued through her several subsequent visits to New York and California.

In between dinners, parties, concerts, and musicales, George, with, as always in Paris, Mabel Schirmer's invaluable help, rushed around looking for the perfect Paris taxi-horn to provide an individual character to his new piece, similar to that which Ross Gorman's clarinet glissando had given to *Rhapsody in Blue,* or the Charleston to *Concerto in F.* He needed a personality that 'said' Paris in the sound. He found it, indeed he found several, in auto-parts stores, and there are photographs of him proudly holding his discoveries in a Paris street.

An American in Paris was to be a ballet suite. He started writing it with no commission but, as usual, as soon as George started playing fragments for friends, even before he left for Europe, it was snapped up by Damrosch for the New York Philharmonic. Later, Diaghilev begged George to allow the Ballet Russes to stage it but George had promised it to Damrosch and he would keep his word.

For the next three months, from March to June 1928, the Gershwin family were ensconced at the Majestic Hotel. A week after they had checked in, two young men knocked, unannounced, on George's door. They were, they explained rather breathlessly, Mario Braggiotti and Jacques Fray, students at the Paris Conservatoire, hoping just to meet their hero. George, with his usual charm and hospitality, invited them in.

Once he realised they could read music, George asked Braggiotti to sight-read the single-line melody in the treble so he could try out an accompaniment. 'And then, for the first time anywhere, there echoed the amazingly original and nostalgic slow movement of *An American in Paris,* undoubtedly one of George's most brilliant works,' recalled Braggiotti. The two 18-year-old students had just heard the 'homesickness' theme, one of the most famous and most evocative melodies in concert music. 'George chewingly switched his perennial cigar from mouth left to mouth right and said, *How do you like it?*'

The boys also got to be the first 'hornists' to try out the taxi horns, which were lying on a table. They all became great friends and George was tremendously helpful to the young duo, hiring them as the pit pianists in the London production of *Funny Face* the following year and becoming their champions when they came to New York to start their American performing career.

Overall the Gershwins had a 'swell' holiday. Frankie got taken up by Elsa Maxwell, the famous 'hostess with the mostest' who gave a Gershwin party at which Frankie sang George and Ira's songs. On this trip Frankie first met Leopold Godowsky, Jr, son of the concert pianist, whom she later married. Almost more importantly at the time, she met Cole Porter, who invited her to stay in Paris to make a special appearance singing George's songs in his new revue *La Revue des Ambassadeurs.* So when the other three Gershwins decamped for Berlin and Vienna in April, Frankie stayed behind in Paris and had the time of her life.

Berlin was full of music and musicians. They met the young Kurt Weill and heard their friend Josefa Rosanka (who had introduced George to Kay Swift Warburg) play at the BechsteinSal. Then they went on to Vienna and the usual over-heated musical atmosphere that exists there even today. Lunch at the Hotel Sacher with Emmerich Kalman was heralded by the restaurant band essaying an excerpt from the *Rhapsody* as they entered and an afternoon with Johann Strauss' widow proved fascinating, even though she tried to sell them a manuscript of *Die Fledermaus* for an exorbitant sum.

George had lunch also with the other famous Viennese operetta composer, Franz Lehár, and his prize pupil, the avant-garde serialist composer Alban Berg. Gershwin and Berg become fast friends. Josefa Rosanka was at that time engaged to Rudolf Kolisch, who invited the two composers to his apartment and, with some colleagues, played a Berg string quartet which fascinated George. Then, it was George's turn. He had a rare moment of shyness. After the intellectual rigour of the Serialist composer, he was reluctant to play show tunes for him but Berg put him at his ease. 'Mr Gershwin,' he said quietly, 'music is music.' George played and Berg loved it.

George returned to Paris to accompany Frankie's debut in *La Revue des Ambassadeurs* and her Gershwin set, said a delighted Mabel Schirmer, 'literally stopped the show'. Frankie thoroughly enjoyed herself, especially with her brother at the keyboard, and was subsequently offered several more roles in Europe but by then she had met Leo Godowsky and both he and George wanted her to return to New York.

The *Concerto in F* had its European premiere that week too with Dimitri Tiomkin (later to become king of Hollywood soundtrack composers) at the piano, and although Prokofiev and Diaghilev and George's old friend, Vladimir Dukelsky (Vernon Duke) were less than enthusiastic about it, the French critics were complimentary and the audiences loved it. As their Paris sojourn drew to a close, it seemed that everyone in the city competed to give the Gershwins the most memorable send-off. It was already May but it embodied the spirit of Vernon Duke's 'April in Paris', the 'charm of Spring' was in the air, the chestnuts were in blossom and this was a feeling none of them would ever reprise. When George left Paris for home his heart did sing. It never occurred to him that he was leaving for the last time.

On the way to the boat, laden with gifts for family and friends, and the complete works of Debussy in eight volumes for himself, George stopped in London to talk with Gertrude Lawrence and Alex Aarons about their new musical, *Treasure Girl*. But it would have to wait until after he had finished *An American in Paris* for the Philharmonic, and made the necessary corrections to *Strike Up the Band*, which, true to his word, Selwyn was preparing for Broadway again.

In the influential magazine *Musical America*, George, when interviewed about *An American in Paris*, is quoted on his influences *(The opening part is developed in typical French style)*, and discusses the importance of 'Les Six', six contemporary French composers who at the time formed a bloc, and of Debussy. George was certainly interested in, and affected by their work, but *An American in Paris* is in fact an intrinsically American view of Paris, a carefree, and above all young, look at a city that to him was always fun, always alive and always beautiful. *My purpose is to portray the impressions of an American visitor in Paris as he strolls about the city, listens to the various street noises and absorbs the French atmosphere.*

An American in Paris is programme music, that is, music designed to tell a story. George's manuscript has a number of markings that indicate where various events occur – 'sees girl . . . meets girl . . . strolling flirtation' – but the best version of the story is the one written by the critic Deems Taylor in the opening night programme which George, of course, approved. He matches each of the themes to an action or emotion of the young American whom we first meet swinging down the Champs Elysées, and headlines each of the major divisions in the piece so a listener has a roadmap to keep him focused throughout the 18-minute piece.

This was George's first concert composition not to include a solo piano and it was all his own work. His orchestration is most original and includes three saxophones, singing trumpets and jazz-style percussion (at one time he considered adding a real jazz drummer but then realised

'You are to imagine . . . an American, visiting Paris, swinging down the Champs-Élysées on a mild sunny morning in May or June. Being what he is, he starts with preliminaries, and is off at full speed at once, to the tune of the first Walking Theme, a straightforward, diatonic air, designed to convey an impression of Gallic freedom and gaiety. Our American's ears being open, as well as his eyes, he notes with pleasure the sounds of the city. French taxicabs seem to amuse him particularly, a fact that the orchestra points out in a brief episode introducing four real Paris taxi horns . . .'

DEEMS TAYLOR'S PROGRAMME NOTE
FOR *AN AMERICAN IN PARIS*

Gene Kelly and Leslie Caron in the film version of An American in Paris 1951

that good orchestra percussionists could handle it.) Although he referred to it as *a rhapsodic ballet,* it had turned into something rather larger, a one-movement descriptive work more usually the province of composers such as Elgar and Richard Strauss. *This new piece,* he told Hyman Sandow, *is written very freely and is the most modern music I've yet attempted.* True, but he's safely in home territory with wide rhapsodic sweeps of melody, clearly differentiated themes, and rhythmic structures that Elgar could never have imagined.

Gone was his original ballet description, although of course at the end of the classic film of the same name, inspired by the music, Gene Kelly and Leslie Caron made cinema history by closing a movie musical with the entire piece, performed as a ballet, with sets and costumes inspired by the Impressionist painters. On the manuscript he is most specific about what he thought it was and this time there was no doubt at all about who had orchestrated it. The title page says:

AN AMERICAN IN PARIS
A Tone Poem for Orchestra

Composed and Orchestrated by George Gershwin

Begun early in 1928. Finished November 18, 1928.

The first Carnegie Hall performance was on 13 December 1928, with the New York Symphonic Society conducted by Walter Damrosch. The audience went wild for it but as usual the reviews were mixed. Some were raves, but even Olin Downes in the *Times*, always a fan, was restrained and some critics were downright vitriolic. When George took Kay to the Saturday performance and they stood at the back of the Hall, he groaned aloud at some of Damrosch's tempi. *Watch out when he bends his knees,* George whispered, *it means he's going to take it too slow.* George read the reviews and stuck them carefully in his scrapbook but he didn't let the negative ones get to him; he was well pleased with his American tourist in the City of Light.

Sweet and Low-Down

I tried to express our manner of living, the tempo of our modern life with its speed and chaos and vitality.   GEORGE GERSHWIN

When the Gershwins returned from Europe in June 1928, their first assignment, before George could concentrate on getting *An American in Paris* ready for its December premiere, was to write the score for the new Gertrude Lawrence musical, *Treasure Girl,* which was due to start rehearsals in August. Fishing once again in the bottomless trunk, they found some lovely songs that were suitable for Gertie's small high voice, including 'I've Got a Crush on You'. Rehearsals went well, there are no reports of Miss Lawrence's usual tantrums, and by October *Treasure Girl* was ready for Philadelphia.

Treasure Girl opened at the Alvin on 8 November and was loathed by critics and audiences alike, Brooks Atkinson calling it, 'an evil thing'. Everything in it was vilified except George and Ira's score but, as Ira pointed out, 'Numbers alone do not make a show.'

What went wrong? Probably the biggest failure was that of Fred Thompson and Vincent Lawrence's book about a girl (Gertie) so avid for money and position that she would even double-cross her lover. This hit all the wrong notes with her audiences, who wanted to love the divine Gertrude Lawrence. *Treasure Girl* lasted for just 68 Broadway performances before being relegated to 'Cain's Warehouse', where scenery from Broadway flops were traditionally stored.

In January 1929 Nat Shilkret, who had conducted the second recording of the *Rhapsody,* got together a *crème de la crème* group of musicians for a radio broadcast of *An American in Paris* and then took it into the recording studio with George in the orchestra doubling on piano and celesta. George made such a nuisance of himself in the early part of the rehearsal that Nat good-naturedly chucked him out while the musicians learnt the piece and then invited him back to play.

The resulting disc is my favourite of all *American in Paris* renderings. It has such energy, its tempi are elastic in the best ways, and

Inextricably bound up with show business in the New York of the Roaring Twenties was organised crime. Prohibition, the outlawing of hard liquor, had made petty criminals of most people. The speakeasies catered to entertainers, businessmen and criminals. Broadway shows were often paid for by crime bosses, buying a show for their latest showgirl girlfriends. Ruby Keeler, who became one of Broadway's biggest musical stars, had been a gangster's girlfriend before she married and it is rumoured that, when he tired of her and she of him, she got him to threaten Al Jolson's life unless he married her, which he did.

it swings, really swings. It contains within it the irrepressible joy of unfettered youth, the simple tale of a young man in Paris; his moods and his homesickness are merely temporary and harmonious clouds crossing the azure-blue sky over Notre Dame.

The big upheaval was domestic. The family at 103rd Street was changing and their needs were changing with it. Rose and Morris wanted to spend their winters in Florida and their summers out of the heat of Manhattan. Arthur, now 29, needed to branch out on his own. He went to work temporarily (this was 1929, remember) on Wall Street while his sister Frankie continued to see Leopold Godowsky Jr. Rose did not approve of Leo, having grander aspirations for her only daughter than a poverty-stricken young violinist, no matter how distinguished his family. (Later, when Leo invented Kodachrome for the Kodak Company, even Rose had to admit she'd been wrong about what kind of a provider her son-in-law would be.) Ira and Lee really wanted a home of their own but George, though he had finally tired of the chaos of a family house, didn't want to be separated from Ira, who represented professional and personal stability.

The solution was simple. They leased two adjoining penthouses in a 17-storey building on Riverside Drive at 75th Street. George's looked west, over the Hudson River, Ira and Lee's south. True to type, Ira's was furnished in traditional style. He and Lee liked antiques, plenty of dark good wood and rich fabrics in deep colours. Just next door, George created one of the grandest Art Deco residences in America. Almost entirely decorated in black and white, with surfaces shiny, the fabrics white-on-white glossy, the wood inlaid and the lighting subtle, this apartment was the last word in contemporary design. Certainly Kay Swift Warburg's taste was much in evidence but George too wanted an elegant and neutral background for his growing gallery of important paintings, which were hung in the new apartment's entertaining rooms, along with a fine landscape by Harry Botkin, George's artist cousin, who had

The Art Deco dining room at Gershwin's Riverside Drive apartment

helped him to build his collection. This was his first home of his own and it reflected his cultivated taste and interests.

Gershwin saw the creative arts as a united whole with the form of expression merely a detail. He once told an interviewer that, *music is design — melody is line; harmony is colour, contrapuntal music is three or four lines forming an abstraction or sometimes a definite shape; dissonance in music is like a distortion in a painting.*

At the same time, George's own painting career blossomed, and he began to be taken seriously by collectors and even an occasional critic. While Ira found painting distracted him from his real creative business of writing lyrics, George found it nourished him, and gave him a form of satisfaction that even his music couldn't. Painting is a solitary act and George was a man who in most circumstances hated to be alone. Even composing, he was happy not only to have Ira working with him, but also, at various times, Mabel, Kay, and others just present in the room while he worked. Painting gave him some much-needed solitude and he continued to develop his skills seriously until he died. His self-portraits open a window into what George Gershwin thought of himself.

He was 30 years old, rich, famous, popular and supremely talented. He had good friends who loved him, a close family, a beautiful home, which was truly his, in a city that was partly his invention, and there seemed to be nothing beyond his grasp. His confidence was sometimes mistaken for conceit but it was not that. He listened to criticism, took seriously the comments of those he respected, sought throughout his life to learn, and never over-estimated his achievements. When he played and replayed his own work it was not out of boastfulness but an almost child-like wonder at what he had wrought and out of his belief that what pleased him would be pleasing to others. Like most undereducated but brilliant men, he needed to know that what he had done was worthy of the attention of others.

He was quite interested in marriage but he was afraid of commitment. Kay was married already and while she always believed that, had George not died young, they would one day have married, the fact that George had happily gone off to Europe without her for months shortly after their affair had started, suggests that he was in no hurry to tie himself to her any more closely than he had already.

His house-warming party at his new apartment at 33 Riverside Drive was, typically, dedicated to those whose help had got him this far – Max Dreyfus, Eva Gauthier, Paul Whiteman, Ferde Grofé, Fred and Adele Astaire, Walter Damrosch, William Daly, Ira and Lee. Their placecards were inscribed with lines from song-lyrics.

In the meantime, there was music to be written. Ziegfeld had remembered that he had the Gershwins under contract for a new Oriental operetta, which had been his idea, *East is West*. Without a great deal of forethought, they had agreed to write it, and in odd moments had completed about half the score. *East is West* never got off the page into a theatre. Ziegfeld did the sums, decided that his original idea was going to be very expensive and suggested (or, rather, demanded) that they write him a score for a newer (cheaper) idea. This was a story about one of his own show-girls to be called, not surprisingly, *Show Girl*. It would go into rehearsal, he informed them, in less than two weeks. Ridiculous, said the Gershwins; no problem, said Ziegfeld, 'Just dig down into the trunk and pull me out a couple of hits.'

When rehearsals began the cast had a script only for the first scene, an outline for some of the rest, and blank spaces where 27 musical items ought to have been. They were still rehearsing the last scene on the train to Boston. The preparations were a shambles but Duke Ellington, whose orchestra was in the pit, was a keen observer, and noticed how unflappable George was and how professional even when his own music was being rudely excised for production reasons:'When cuts and adjustments were being made . . . you would never guess he was the great George Gershwin'.

Show Girl opened on 24 June. All the auguries were right and

On the opening night of *Show Girl*, Al Jolson, husband of the leading lady, Ruby Keeler, carried out a bizarre publicity stunt during her best number, 'Liza'. *Imagine the audience's surprise and mine,* George recalled, *when without warning Al Jolson, who was sitting in the third row on the aisle, jumped up and sang a chorus of 'Liza' to his bride.* Jolson had cooked up the scheme with Ziegfeld to draw attention to the show and himself. It worked well enough that he went on doing it periodically throughout the run. The song was never thereafter associated with Keeler, but Jolson sang it until the end of his life.

the creative team was the cream of show business. This was a Florenz Ziegfeld production with a book adapted by J P McEvoy from his own novel, music by George Gershwin with lyrics by Ira and Gus Kahn, the Duke Ellington Orchestra in the pit, designs by Joseph Urban, and, by any standards, an amazing cast. An entire troupe of ballet dancers were also included to dance *An American in Paris* (hastily co-opted into the score).

Show Girl opened in New York in July but by August it was clear that it wouldn't do and Ziegfeld closed it in September, typically blaming everybody else for *Show Girl's* failure at the box office. He refused to pay royalties for the score and for the first and only time, George tried to sue a producer.

Meanwhile, also in August, George made his conducting debut, leading the New York Philharmonic at Lewisohn Stadium in *An American in Paris*. He practiced with the Nat Shilkret recording in front of a mirror until he and his old teacher Edward Kilenyi, drafted in to teach him conducting technique, were satisfied. By performance night he was gesture-perfect and the Stadium set new attendance records. The packed audience was treated to a double – George Gershwin playing *Rhapsody in Blue* as piano soloist, and then, after the interval, conducting *An American in Paris*.

The critics were enthusiastic, the audience even more so, and George had a wonderful time. He loved the idea of controlling his own tempi, of deciding exactly how his music should sound without having to convey his intentions through a conductor. Hereafter he would conduct in the concert hall whenever he was asked and he frequently led the pit orchestra in the opening nights of his musicals.

George's suit against Ziegfeld failed for the saddest of reasons: by now it was October 1929, the Stock Market Crash had happened, and Ziegfeld had been completely ruined. Had the judge decided in George's favour, there would have been no money to pay him.

Strike Up the Band · 1929 - 1933

'Gershwin Shelves Jazz For Opera' NY WORLD HEADLINE, OCTOBER 1929

It is impossible to overestimate the effect of the Stock Market Crash
on the economy and psyche of America. Rich men jumped out of
Wall Street windows, unable to face the possibility of life without
their fortunes, and millions of poor and middle-class men with
families, who had worked all their lives, formed lines in the street
for handouts of food and clothing. A nation built on confidence
quite simply lost its nerve, its identity, its sense of itself, rather
as it did again in the wake of the destruction of the World Trade
Center on 11 September 2001. If it was no longer the thrusting,
teeming, successful hope of the world, what was it? For the rest of
George's life, America was trying to find out.

Entertainment suffered less than almost any other industry.
People needed to enjoy themselves amidst the horrors around
them. George, insulated by his talent and his wealth, nevertheless saw the terrible havoc of lives destroyed, families wrecked,
and sales of his friends' possessions at firesale prices. The light-
heartedness and hedonism that had characterised the 20s and had
made New York the shining Art Deco banner of the New World,
had gone, if not forever, certainly until after World War Two. It
was a time for serious endeavours and George was ready to try
something new and more substantive.

Although he had denied it in several interviews, George had
become fascinated by the possibility of writing an opera. Now
he became interested in *The Dybbuk,* a traditional Jewish folk

tale about demonic possession that had recently been produced as a play both in Yiddish and in an English translation by Henry Aalsberg. It was suggested to him that this story of a restless spirit who inhabits the body of a young girl would make a grand opera in all senses of the word 'grand'.

He had a number of conversations with Aalsberg, who was to be his librettist, planned to take as much as a year out to study Jewish music and rhythm, and even got as far as a contract with the Met, which offered $1,000 for a year's work, to be shared with Aalsberg. After several successful years, he could afford to work for so little and he was keen to see if he was capable of composing a full-length opera. Finally, though, the project was scuppered not by money, but because an Italian composer had already been granted the musical rights. So that was that, but from now on the idea of an opera was never far from the front of George's mind.

If many musicals of the period failed because their books were too insubstantial, the first version of *Strike Up the Band* had failed, at least in part, because George S Kaufman's anti-war, anti-big business, anti-politicians script was too intellectually demanding, too acerbic and too sharp. Now producer Edgar Selwyn, sure that he had a really entertaining and important musical in there somewhere, was determined to prove it.

To soften the script without destroying its values, he added Morrie Ryskind to the writing team. Morrie had worked with Kaufman before on an

Strike Up The Band was better the second time around

Irving Berlin revue for the Marx Brothers, *Animal Crackers,* and was able to add some leavening to the original 1927 book. It was still funny, still challenging, but now the toughest of the jokes were turned into a dream sequence, which softened the blackness of the comedy.

There is no doubt that George and Ira excelled themselves in *Strike Up the Band.* Ira's lyrics have that crystal clarity and precision that caused him to be referred to by his peers as 'the Jeweller' and George's music went much further than simply setting notes to lyrics. George and Ira's usual method of collaboration involved George playing a tune that Ira hummed around the house until he had an idea for a lyric and then they would find a way of interpolating it into whatever plot they were working on. Here they worked differently, adhering closely to Ryskind and Kaufman's script and writing every song according to the mood and focus of that moment in the plot. The action was therefore advanced by words, by music, by movement or by a combination of all three. There are no conventional 'take-out' songs in this score at all. It was, long before Sondheim, the first musically integrated musical and, in recognition of that, the score was published as a whole, not just as individual songs.

Strike Up the Band in its second incarnation was, it is clear from the existing photographs and scraps of rehearsal film, great fun for all its creative team. George was present at rehearsals, often playing for them (the scrap of film I referred to in the Introduction comes from a chorus line-up for this show) and his enthusiasm was infectious.

He had also decided, with his newfound confidence as a symphony orchestra conductor, to lead the pit orchestra on opening night. His first biographer, Isaac Goldberg, who was there, described George's delight: 'To watch him at rehearsals is to see with what ease he gets the best out of his men with the baton. Baton, did I say? George conducts with a baton, with his cigar, with his shoulders, with his hips, with his eyes, with what not. He sings with the principals and the chorus; he whistles; he imitates the various instruments of the orchestra.'

The score includes 'Soon', 'I've Got a Crush on You' (rescued from *Treasure Girl*) and, of course, the irresistible title march. 'Strike Up the Band', was the fifth melody George had written for this place in the show and it became one of his most popular. The show opened on Broadway on 14 January 1930 to a barrage of blissful reviews. It ran for 191 performances. After a few less than inspiring recent shows – *Treasure Girl, Show Girl,* and the aborted *East is West* – the Gershwins had another honest-to-God smash hit.

With hardly time to take a breath after the opening of *Strike Up the Band,* the brothers were on to their next show: *Girl Crazy.* No fewer than three of the greatest songs ever written come from *Girl Crazy.* It made Broadway stars of two all-time major performers and such was the quality of the talent overall that even the pit orchestra was arguably the best ever. The usual slender musical comedy story (by Guy Bolton and John McGowan) was of a young Manhattan playboy sent to the Wild West by a strict father, there to fall in love with the local postmistress.

The cast featured two young girls called Virginia McMath and Ethel Zimmerman, both in their first starring Broadway roles, and both destined for glory. By the time Virginia was cast as the postmistress she had been invited to the Riverside Drive penthouse and George had played for her a song that he said, almost certainly untruthfully, he had written for her. The refrain began, 'They're writing songs of love, but not for me.' That year she took her stepfather's surname coupled with the nickname given by a tiny cousin who couldn't pronounce 'Virginia', dyed her hair from blonde to flame, and was reborn as Ginger Rogers.

Fred Astaire and Ginger Rogers take notes from Gershwin at the piano

The other kid, Ethel Zimmerman, had until then only sung at weddings and bar mitzvahs. George's producer and old friend Vinton Freedley had heard her by accident and he brought her to the apartment on Riverside Drive to sing for George. This small self-possessed girl opened her mouth and a stunned Gershwin told her, *Don't ever go near a teacher, he'll only ruin you.* Her voice was like a bell, clear and accurate, with a head-tone of pure steel.

From that moment there was no doubt that she would be cast in *Girl Crazy,* nor that she would sing several solo numbers. George played them for her and, with the respect he habitually showed to those with true talent, the star composer told the unknown young woman gently that if there was anything in the songs she didn't like, he'd be happy to change them for her. The song he played was 'I Got Rhythm'. Overwhelmed, the girl whispered that the songs would do nicely, just the way they were. 'To me it was like meeting God,' she said later. 'Imagine the great Gershwin playing his songs for me . . . No wonder I was tongue-tied . . . Whatever I said, I meant it to be grateful and humble.'

In *Girl Crazy,* Ginger also got to sing the hit of the show, 'Embraceable You', while Ethel had 'Sam and Delilah', a parody of 'Frankie and Johnnie', and 'What Love Has Done To Me'. In her memoirs, entitled *Who Could Ask For Anything More?* from the punchline in 'I Got Rhythm', Ethel rather acidly describes Ginger Rogers as she was then: 'Ginger was pretty and could sing and dance but nobody would ever call her 'The Voice'; she sang charmingly, but her songs never required real power.' True, the power was all in the songs written for The Voice – also often known as The Golden Foghorn – Miss Ethel (Zim) Merman herself.

One more footnote for historians of the musical. Fred Astaire, who otherwise had nothing to do with the show, dropped into rehearsals one day to visit George and ended up choreographing a number for Ginger. Thus it was that the first time Fred and Ginger danced arm in arm, if not cheek to cheek, was during the rehearsals for *Girl Crazy.*

The rest of the cast was equally fine, with Allan Kearns as the NY playboy who turns Custerville, Arizona into Sin City, Willie Howard, and William Kent. Unusually for the time, George had finagled an augmented pit orchestra and what a pit orchestra it was! Jack Teagarden, Glenn Miller, Benny Goodman, Gene Krupa, Red Nichols and Jimmy Dorsey, all jazzmen who would lead their own major jazz ensembles, were under George Gershwin's baton in that pit. Of all the nights of all the shows in the era before Original Cast Recordings were even considered, that *Girl Crazy* opening night in 1930 is the one I wish most fervently that someone had recorded.

It opened at the Alvin Theatre on 14 October 1930 and ran for 272 performances, their most commercially successful musical since *Lady, Be Good!* The notices were fine, especially for the two new stars and the Gershwins' score. George wrote to Goldberg:

Ethel Merman in Annie Get Your Gun

The show looks so good that I can leave in a few weeks for Hollywood, with the warm feeling that I have a hit under my belt.

George and Ira (with Lee, of course, and Guy Bolton) were due to leave for California on 5 November and their parents were off to the Florida sunshine on Sunday 2 November. When Leo Godowsky returned to New York on 1 November, he realised that, if he and Frankie wanted to marry in the presence of their families, it would have to be on the following day or not for months. He had already waited for nearly two years, hoping to overcome the dislike of Rose Gershwin but her opposition to their marriage showed no sign of abating.

Leo and Frankie scrambled around, getting a marriage license, finding a rabbi, buying a ring, and attending to the 1001 details that usually a girl and her mother take months to accomplish. Frankie was denied all the fun of being a bride-to-be by her mother's objections, her father's indifference, and her brothers' self-absorption.

Lee allowed her and Ira's penthouse to be used for the ceremony and a few friends straggled in. George wandered in from next door in his pyjamas (how long would it have taken him to go back across his terrace and get dressed?) to play the Wedding March and, inevitably, most of *Rhapsody in Blue,* to the delight of the rabbi, who claimed to be a music-lover. Morris's reaction on being told that his only daughter was to be married that after-noon was that he and Rose would have to be sure they didn't miss the 6pm train to Florida (were there no later trains they could have taken instead?) and Rose was Rose, subsequently attributing many well-timed last-minute asthma attacks to her daughter's choice of husband. There is no record of any member of the family giving Frankie or Leo any kind of wedding present.

It was rather a sad affair, this wedding, saved only by the intervention of outsiders. Frankie only had flowers because Kay Swift had turned up with the gift of a bouquet for Rose's journey, and the bridal couple only had a reception because Gertie Lawrence and her current man Bert Taylor were giving a going-away party anyway for George and Ira and no preparation was needed to turn it into a wedding party.

For a family that seemed so close, this was not one of the shining moments in Gershwin history and reflected badly on all of them. It demonstrated once and for all, if demonstration were needed, that George was by now in every way the Favourite Son, followed closely by the other boys and that Frankie was nowhere. Frankie's marriage to Leo was prosperous, happy and lasted until their deaths.

Who cares?

You know, the old artistic soul must be appeased every so often.

GEORGE GERSHWIN IN A LETTER TO ISAAC GOLDBERG

George, Ira and Lee moved into Greta Garbo's old house in Beverly Hills. *Sleeping in the bed that she used,* George wrote to Goldberg, *hasn't helped my sleep any.* They were there to work on *Delicious,* starring Janet Gaynor and Charles Farrell and produced by Winford Sheehan. Set mostly in Manhattan, it allowed the Gershwins to salvage at least one song from the trunk, write half a dozen new ones, an extended dream sequence and, inevitably, a rhapsody, first known as *Manhattan Rhapsody,* then as *Rhapsody in Rivets.*

They stayed for three months, went to some good parties, took a trip to Mexico, and George had a very satisfactory interlude with the silent screen star, Aileen Pringle. Although they had wanted to stay in Hollywood for the filming of *Delicious* they found they couldn't spare the time because at the end of February they were contracted to begin work on a new political satire, *Of Thee I Sing* and for that, they had to be back on Riverside Drive. They decided to go home for *Of Thee I Sing,* and return to Hollywood later to watch the shooting of *Delicious.* As it turned out, however, although Morrie Ryskind and George Kaufman had written a 14-page treatment for the show, they were being glacially slow about turning it into a real script from which George and Ira could work.

Back in Manhattan, George used the time to expand *Manhattan Rhapsody in Rivets* from the *Delicious* score into what would become the *Second Rhapsody.* He didn't have a commission for it but, while he waited for the script for *Of Thee I Sing,* he did have the time. There was the additional advantage that, with no commission, there was no deadline so he could work at his own speed, knowing that it wasn't to be immediately premiered like his other concert works and that there was no conductor waiting to programme it for his orchestra.

He worked diligently through the spring, first expanding the movie theme into a full-blown composition, then on a two-piano reduction, finally on the full orchestration, until, at the end of June, he hired 55 musicians to try out his new *Second Rhapsody for Orchestra with Piano* (a title he felt was 'more dignified' than his original working title at the NBC Studios). The result, a delighted George wrote to Goldberg, was *most gratifying. In many respects, such as orchestration and form, it is the best thing I've written.*

With his usual enthusiasm for new technology, George persuaded the Victor Recording Company to make a test recording of the work, so that he could replay it to discover whatever small changes might be necessary. While other composers shunned the rapid advances of recording techniques, Gershwin embraced them. In return, the record companies competed to record his music, making George Gershwin one of the engines that drove the juggernaut of change from live to recorded music.

Once the *Rhapsody* was in the form he wanted it, and George had sent the final version to the copyist, however, he was at a loose end. The filming of *Delicious* was disastrously behind schedule, so his planned second trip to Hollywood was delayed, and Aarons and Freedley, his long-time producers, had so far failed to come up with the book of the new show (eventually called *Pardon My English*) he was committed to write for them. He played some golf, bought some paintings, dated a vast selection of pretty but inconsequential girls, wrote to his distant cousin and dear friend Rosamund Walling in London, briefly gave up smoking his beloved cigars in an effort to cure his 'composer's stomach', and fretted. George Gershwin unemployed was George Gershwin unhappy.

Things are very depressing around here, he wrote to George Pallay. *All my relations are in terrible shape. There is not a rich one in a carload. I'm trying my best to do what I can but it isn't very pleasant.* Pallay, afraid George was running out of money, offered to lend him some but George refused, saying that he was just feeling short because, *I'm not used to having months go by without those weekly checks coming in.*

As his patience with Aarons and Freedley was frayed by their apparent inability to find a book for him to work with, George even briefly considered becoming his own producer. Many of his fellow composers, notably Irving Berlin, managed their own shows. But George was no businessman and, on reflection, he realised that it was hard enough to compose the music to order, on time and with the appropriate mood and length, without adding the financial responsibility of the entire production as well.

By September Ryskind and Kaufman had worked some real

magic and what they had written had been worth the wait. He wrote to Rosamund, who had been expecting him to visit her, that he was working with Ira on *a George Kaufman book – a satire on Politics and Love – called* Of Thee I Sing. *It is most amusing and we are looking forward to writing a score for it.*

Ryskind and Kaufman had cast their net wide, reeled in almost all of their favourite targets – the labryinthine workings of the White House, the unimportance of the office of Vice President,

Gershwin and Sergey Koussevitzky

the idiocies of beauty contests, the French, marriage, babies, and political manoeuvoring – and taken potshots at them all. It was scabrously funny and coruscatingly accurate in its potshots at authority and its sour, sideways view of public and private life. George, with his vast experience, knew that this was stage comedy writing of a very high order.

The score that George and Ira wrote owes much to and has always been compared with Gilbert and Sullivan's operettas, particularly *The Pirates of Penzance,* but it is more surreal, and certainly more American in its breadth and ambition. The Gershwins weren't trying for individual hits that could be lifted from the show and played on the radio. The style of Ira's lyrics was indistinguishable from Ryskind and Kaufman's book, while George's music was so integrated into the text that it was often several moments before the audience was aware that the actors had made the transition from dialogue to song.

They opened in Boston on 8 December and, once the local critics had their say, the entire run was sold out on a wave of euphoria which word-of-mouth carried to New York. On 26 December 1931 at the Music Box Theatre on Broadway, George Gershwin was the pit conductor for the New York opening night of *Of Thee I Sing.* The audience and critical response were ecstatic. George Jean Nathan wrote that *Of Thee I Sing* was 'a landmark in American satirical musical comedy'. In the *Times,* Brooks Atkinson raved that 'Mr Gershwin pours music out in full measure and in many voices . . . Mr Gershwin is exuberant . . . He not only has ideas but enthusiasm . . . Satire needs . . . the virtuosity of Mr Gershwin's music . . . it has the depth of artistry and the glow and pathos of comedy.'

Ira was now one of the backers, having been convinced by Kaufman to invest $2,500 for 5 per cent of the show, which, as it turned out, made him a profit of more than 300 per cent. The money he invested, though, was George's. Owing to the Depression, Ira was a bit short.

Of Thee I Sing, the Gershwins' most successful show, ran for 441 performances. Morrie Ryskind, George Kaufman, and Ira Gershwin would win the 1932 Pulitzer Prize for Drama for the book and lyrics but this was before there was a Pulitzer Prize for Music and George's name was not mentioned. George declared it to be *one of those rare shows where everything clicked,* added that it was *the one show that I'm more proud of than any I have written,* and enjoyed the resumption of the weekly cheques.

It was eight months from the completion of the *Second Rhapsody* to its first public performance except, of course, at parties where George and his by now ubiquitous friend, Oscar Levant, played the two-piano reduction whenever there was a second piano. While he was in Boston with the out-of-town *Of Thee I Sing,* George had met the pioneering conductor of the Boston Symphony, Serge Koussevitsky, who had offered him a commission to write a composition for the 50th anniversary season of the orchestra. At the time, George had been too busy fine-tuning his show to accept. Once *Of Thee I Sing* had opened on Broadway, however, and George had had time to think about it, he offered Koussevitsky and the Boston Symphony the *Second Rhapsody*. As it turned out, it was an inspired choice. Serge Koussevitsky was extremely interested in modern music and had given Aaron Copland his first symphonic performances. On 29 January 1932, in Symphony Hall, Boston, the *Second Rhapsody* was first heard by a paying audience and only a few days later, on 5 February, it arrived in New York's Carnegie Hall.

The critic Olin Downes said, not without justice, that it was 'too long for its material', while others found it well crafted (some of his previous concert works had been thought either technically slapdash or heavily doctored by someone else) and all agreed with George that this was his most fully realised concert work. Nobody, this time, accused him of not having completed the piece himself. There was a general perception, however , that it lacked either the originality and brilliance of *Rhapsody in Blue* or the instant accessibility of *An American in Paris*.

What perhaps all but the most perceptive listeners at the time missed was the *Second Rhapsody*'s interior darkness. This is, by far, the hardest-edged and most jagged Gershwin concert piece. It is, in hindsight, a piece essentially of the 1930s rather than the 1920s. Leaving behind the romanticism and hedonism of the 1920s, it reflects not only the jumpiness of Art Deco architecture, with its sharp corners and high, uneven projections that were at exactly that moment shaping the new New York skyline, but also the poverty of its streets. The Depression was at its height and there seemed then to be no end to the meanness and misery of unemployment, and the despair of an economy that could not find its way back up.

The *Second Rhapsody* is gritty, realistic, and often confrontational. It summarises Gershwin's mastery over the orchestra – he uses

The classic Gershwin profile with cigar

his instruments in unusual but entirely defensible ways – and demonstrates his willingness and ability to express what he saw around him instead of what he wished were there.

Not entirely surprisingly, then, the *Second Rhapsody* has never achieved the standard repertoire status of the other concert works, although it is now increasingly to be found on major orchestral programmes or in its two-piano version where it surprises listeners (expecting 'Fascinating Rhythm' or 'Embraceable You') with its melancholy and anger.

George was tired after the relentless work of getting *Of Thee I Sing* opened at the Music Box, and the *Second Rhapsody* safely launched at Boston's Symphony and New York's Carnegie Halls, so a holiday was in order. He went to Cuba with a group of non-musical friends. As he wrote to George Pallay, *I spent two hysterical weeks in Havana where no sleep was had but the quantity and quality of the fun made up for that.* He also acquired several authentic Cuban instruments in order, he said, that he could write a rumba, and enjoyed the attention of numerous local musicians who, on hearing who was staying at the hotel, serenaded him *en masse* at four in the morning, to the irritation of other hotel guests.

Aarons had finally come up with the book of *Pardon My English,* to which both George and Ira were contractually committed, and they immediately started work on that. The producer, Sam Harris, buoyed by the success of *Of Thee I Sing,* was talking about a sequel, and George had also promised to write a new concert work, his promised rumba, for an all-Gershwin concert to be given that August at Lewinsohn Stadium. If all that weren't enough, at the beginning of May Random House published, in a limited edition, *George Gershwin's Song Book,* a compilation of 18 of his songs, with the original sheet music and George's own subsequently developed variations, complete with his own commentary. He wrote this himself, dedicated it to Kay Swift, and proved himself an insightful and elegant music writer. He was once again over-committed, a state in which he thrived.

Sadly, at the same time, he was very much affected by the death, from leukaemia, of his father. Morris had been ill for some time and died on 14 May 1932. An hour before he died, with the sense of humour that had nurtured his family through good times and bad, he teased Rose that now, finally, she could marry a tall man as she had always wanted. She never remarried.

As ever, Gershwin was looking for a teacher to fill in the gaps that he and others perceived in his musical education. When, in 1929, Russian composer Alexander Glazunov had said of *Rhapsody in Blue,* 'It is part human and part animal', and went on to berate George for knowing nothing about theory, George asked him with whom he could study. From various sources the name Joseph Schillinger, the most famous professor of music theory of his time, emerged and in this crowded spring of 1932, George Gershwin, perhaps the most famous living composer of his time, humbly presented himself for lessons. Vladimir Drozdoff, a Russian composer-pianist who had worked with Alexander Glazunov before emigrating to the United States said: 'Though Gershwin was a very famous man even in the 20s, he had the strength and wisdom that accepts criticism and goes on learning.'

Schillinger's rigour suited George's restless nature and, according to Schillinger, they met about three times a week (although where he found the time is unclear) for the next four years. Today he'd probably have gone to a psychoanalyst instead' although eventually he did that too. The methodology, according to Oscar Levant who also studied with Schillinger, was mathematical rather than musical, and highly cerebral. It is understandable that an autodidact such as George would have been enthralled by the intellectual musicological puzzles posed by such a method. If Schillinger lacked originality and creativity, George already had plenty of those qualities himself. These studies fed, at the very least, a psychological need in George to stretch himself and to explore his own potential.

Under the considerable influence of Joseph Schillinger, Gershwin wrote his *Rumba* using his riotously acquired Cuban instruments just in time for the all-Gershwin concert at Lewisohn Stadium. This performance was a smash-hit, a kind of survey of his career to date, including both his concert and show music, and it must have displayed, definitively, if proof were needed, that there was really no difference between them, just a deepening and maturing of technique and inspiration which applied to both. The stadium was a sell-out, an audience of 18,000 with, reportedly, thousands more turned away. Gershwin called it *the most exciting night I have ever had.* Part of this concert was repeated in November in a benefit for the out-of-work musicians of the Musicians' Symphony Orchestra, including *Rumba,* now retitled *Cuban Overture.*

One Allan Langley, a minor composer who happened to be playing at the concert, got it into his head that William Daly, who was conducting, had actually composed Gershwin's *Four Tunes,* a medley of popular songs George had arranged for the Stadium concert. A particularly nasty little article by Langley duly appeared in *The American Spectator,* which was summarily and humorously repudiated by Daly in the much larger circulation *New York Times.* Typically, George himself disdained to dignify the accusation with either a denial or a lawsuit, both of which were urged on him. 'Why bother?' was his only comment.

Pardon My English, the Gershwins' new musical for Aarons and Freedley, was a disaster. The long-awaited book was a dreadful piece of work and the resulting show included only one really fine song, the beautifully under-stated 'Isn't it a Pity?' Suffice to say that it ran for a scant five weeks and Ira never even listed the songs in

'I suppose I should really resent the fact that Langley attributes Gershwin's work to me, since Langley finds all of it so bad. But fortunately for my *amour propre,* I have heard some of Langley's compositions. He really should stay away from ink and stick to the viola . . . [Gershwin] receives many . . . suggestions from his many friends to whom he always plays his various compositions, light or symphonic, while they are in the process of being written. Possibly Mr Langley feels that we all get together (and we'd have to meet in the Yankee Stadium) and write Mr Gershwin's music for him.'

WILLIAM DALY RESPONDS TO
ALLAN LANGLEY'S ACCUSATIONS

his catalogue. Freedley left town owing a great deal of money and Aarons, who had been George's most frequent producer since the beginning of both their careers, never produced again.

George and Ira's next, *Let Them Eat Cake,* the sequel to their greatest hit, *Of Thee I Sing,* although a much stronger show, suffered nearly the same fate. It took potshots at just about everything, not saving its brickbats for war, as in *Strike Up the Band,* or politics as in *Of Thee I Sing.* Ira wrote later, 'Kaufman and Ryskind's libretto was at times extremely witty – at other times unrelentingly realistic in its criticism of the then American scene.'

Overall, audiences liked *Let Them Eat Cake* at least as well as *Of Thee I Sing* but the times were very different. Audiences seeing the rise of Hitler in Germany and surveying the depression and unemployment at home were less likely to laugh at the political shambles portrayed in the new show, less willing to forgive the incompetence of the fictional Wintergreen Administration, and less sure that 'it couldn't happen here'.

They were all disappointed when *Let Them Eat Cake* didn't work. It opened in Boston in September and on Broadway in October at the Imperial, and it ran for only 90 performances, better than *Pardon My English,* to be sure, but a flop nonetheless.

With the optimism that characterised him, George decided to move house that year – apparently his art collection was outgrowing his wall-space in Riverside Drive. 132 East 72nd Street had a 14-room two-storey apartment which took his fancy. He had a studio to paint in and a double-height living room, but his pride and joy was his workroom, with its two Steinway grand pianos and a specially built desk that included, amongst other contemporary wonders, a retractable pencil sharpener. As at Riverside Drive, the paintings which arrived from Europe at regular intervals were hung and re-hung in a display which now rivalled the best private collections of modern art in the world. Inevitably, Ira and Lee moved in across the street.

I Loves You, Porgy · 1933 - 1935

'I think that he is probably the only white man in America who could have done that.' DUBOSE HEYWARD

George had first read DuBose Heyward's bestselling novel *Porgy*, the story of a crippled beggar in a poor black fishing community in Charleston, South Carolina, in 1926 and had written to him to suggest that they collaborate on an operatic adaptation of it. Although Heyward's response was immediate and positive, the project had been delayed several times, primarily because Dorothy Heyward had adapted the novel into a play, which was produced successfully by the Theatre Guild in 1927. After that the timing was somehow never quite right because both men had contractual obligations to other work and their free time never coincided.

As usual when enthusiastic, George told everybody of his interest in the work and everyone he told agreed that a grand opera was the logical next Gershwin step. Even the Metropolitan Opera had offered $5,000 to mount the premiere but George turned them down on the grounds that he wanted a wider audience for Porgy than would have been possible in the standard opera house repertoire system where a new opera is typically performed only two or three times a week for one season only.

A week after *Let Them Eat Cake* opened on Broadway in October 1933, George signed a contract with the Theatre Guild to write the music for an opera based on Heyward's book. It was not quite as odd in the 30s as it would be today for a New York Jew to collaborate with a white Southerner on a work based on black peasant life but it was odd enough. The only black music familiar to opera-going Northerners was a blues-derived jazz, which seemed light-years away from an operatic vocabulary, and the patois of the novel's dialogue seemed at first glance to be inimical to a serious music setting, but George and Heyward liked one another and invented a productive partnership that gave birth to the first truly American grand opera. (Yes, Scott Joplin's *Treemonisha* was composed earlier but it was not produced in its intended form until the 1970s.)

On many levels *Porgy* was a brave choice for George – he didn't know the territory, he had had little contact with black people who were not well-known musicians and (outside of jazz) knew nothing of their culture. His musical vocabulary was unfailingly urban and urbane, his humour was Northern and sophisticated, and none of his characters had ever been poor except by choice. *Porgy* was as far from his own experience as was imaginable in America but something in those poverty-stricken black Gullah people of South Carolina spoke to him.

DuBose Heyward was his secret weapon. Though white and from an upper-class family fallen on hard times, DuBose knew the Charleston waterfront intimately, having been a cotton checker there as a young man. Self-educated, he knew the people and how they spoke, what they felt, where their loyalties lay, and what and whom they feared. Among Heyward's varied and colourful acquaintance, when he and his wife Dorothy lived

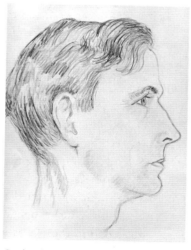

Gershwin's own drawing of Dubose Heyward

in Cabbage Row (the prototype for Catfish Row, *Porgy's* setting), was Samuel Smalls, a beggar who, having lost the use of his legs, would wheel himself around on a goat cart, hence his nickname, Goat Sammy. A chance newspaper item about him gave DuBose an idea. He realised that Goat Sammy, 'the object of public charity by day, had a private life of his own by night. It was a tempestuous life and in it were the seeds of human struggle that make for drama.' In this mostly imaginary 'tempestuous life' Heyward had found his Porgy, or Porgo, as he was called in the first draft.

Tentatively, over a period of many months from about September 1932, George and DuBose began to exchange ideas, meeting occasionally, sometimes with Ira. Mostly, though, they wrote letters in which they explored their approach to the adaptation. In December 1933, George decided to go to Charleston for the first time. All their other meetings had been in New York or on the road. In advance, he told his host, DuBose, what he wanted: *I would like to see the town, hear some spirituals, and perhaps go to a coloured café or two.*

The project had almost been derailed when Al Jolson, still a big star, offered to buy the rights to *Porgy* from Heyward. Jolson wanted Jerome Kern and Oscar Hammerstein II to create a star vehicle in which Jolson could play the title role, blacked-up. George did not try to stand in Heyward's way, but he did not want anything to do with a Jolson star vehicle, even if Jolson had offered it to him. He saw *Porgy* as serious music, definitely an opera, not an operetta or a musical play, and certainly not a popular musical comedy. In the end, when Kern and Hammerstein proved unavailable, Jolson lost interest.

DuBose Heyward later wrote of their research trips: '. . . the interesting discovery to me, as we sat listening to their spirituals, or watched a group shuffling before a cabin or a country store was that to George it was more like a homecoming than an exploration. The quality in him that had produced the

George and Ira Gershwin with Dubose Heyward in Boston 1935

Rhapsody in Blue in the most sophisticated city in America, found its counterpart in the impulse behind the music and bodily rhythms of the simple Negro peasant of the South.'

At the same time, George was involved in composing a new concert work, *Variations on 'I Got Rhythm'*, for a concert tour that George undertook as a payoff for a longtime debt. Harry Askins, the tour manager, was an old friend from his time at Remick's, who had introduced George to his original publisher Max Dreyfus, so when he suggested a 28-day, 28-city, 28-concert all-Gershwin tour, George agreed. It was a financial disaster and cost George several thousand dollars because Askins had booked them into towns and venues often far too small to cover the large orchestra, soloists and conductors' fees. But George, gracious as ever, told Heyward that it had been, *a very worthwhile thing for me to have done and I have many pleasant memories.*

While on tour George had sketched out the beginnings of 'Summertime' and several other themes for *Porgy,* but then, when he returned to New York, his work on the opera was again interrupted by the introduction of his new weekly radio programme. In *Music by Gershwin* he played his music (and that of his friends and contemporaries) and talked with them about his songs, to the delight of his sponsor, laxative manufacturer Feen-a-Mint. Two further series of *Music by Gershwin* followed.

Even while working on other projects, he continued to work on *Porgy* in every free moment. Summertime was best. For July and August 1934, George and his artist cousin, Henry (Harry) Botkin, decamped to Folly Island, 10 miles from Charleston and, as George wrote to his mother, *Imagine, there's not one telephone on the whole island – public or private.* They lived in a primitive shack on the beach, wearing as little as possible and sporting straggling beards, their only concession to George's normal life being a rickety upright piano.

DuBose showed them where they could hear authentic Gullah music and the spirituals which would underpin the score. The local residents, island people uncontaminated by the cities and exposure to other cultures, were closer to Africa than almost any other American blacks except possibly those who inhabit the Georgia Sea Islands. This direct African influence can still be experienced in what they call 'shouting', a complex set of rhythms beaten out with hands and feet which accompany church singing.

George, rhythmic innovator that he was, was fascinated by 'shouting'. DuBose vividly wrote later: 'I shall never forget the night when, at a Negro meeting on a remote sea island, George started 'shouting' with them. And, eventually, to their huge delight, stole the show from their champion 'shouter'. I think that he is probably the only white man in America who could have done that.'

Porgy, soon and forever after to be known as *Porgy and Bess* so as not to confuse it with Dorothy Heyward's play (and because it seemed properly operatic to George, fitting in with his notion of *Tristan und Isolde* and *Pelléas et Mélisande*), was composed over a period of 20 months in a variety of places from the South Carolina beach shack to Emil Mosbacher's various palatial homes in Florida, upstate New York and Shelter Island, to George's own palatial home on East 72nd. By the time he had finished the orchestration, on 2 September 1935, there were more than 700 pages of manuscript with a running time of approximately four and a half hours.

Throughout the writing process, George and DuBose worked by letter, occasional telephone calls, and even more occasional meetings. It was DuBose, who knew that his refusal to work away from his South Carolina home was impeding the lyric writing, who suggested that Ira should share the lyrics credit. So, when he had fulfilled his commitment to the *Follies of 1936,* Ira joined them, by which time they had finished Act One, which is why none of Ira's lyrics appear there.

DuBose described the process: 'We evolved a system by which, between my visits North, or George's dash to Charleston, I could set scenes and lyrics. Then the brothers Gershwin, after their extraordinary fashion, would get at the piano, pound, wrangle,

'My first impression of my collaborator remains with me and is singularly vivid. A young man of enormous physical and emotional vitality, who possessed the faculty of seeing himself quite impersonally and realistically, and who knew exactly what he wanted and where he was going. This characteristic put him beyond both modesty and conceit. About himself he would merely mention certain facts, aspirations, failings . . .'

DUBOSE HEYWARD

burst into weird snatches of song, and eventually emerge with polished lyrics.' While there were plenty of lively discussions about all manner of dramatic and musical issues on *Porgy and Bess* there is not one recorded quarrel between the collaborators – surely a record.

Kay Swift was undoubtedly invaluable in the process of notating the opera as was Stephan Zoltai, George's copyist. At this distance in time it is impossible to know how great was the help or influence of the teacher, Joseph Schillinger, who subsequently claimed a huge but unsubstantiated share of the credit.

The Theatre Guild were perfect producers. Not only did they put up all the money, discouraging additional offers of backing (as usual, however, George and Ira had a stake in the production), they also relinquished all casting and production decisions to the collaborators. They did, however, suggest rather strongly that Rouben Mamoulian, a major New York theatre director who had directed *Porgy* the play, should serve as both producer and director for the opera. George was in favour, knowing that Mamoulian was intensely musical and would never sacrifice musical quality for a production or dramatic effect.

George and Ira sang themselves hoarse playing the score for Rouben one night. His recollection of the two brothers together was one to cherish: 'George was the orchestra and played the parts. Ira sang the other half . . . It was touching to see how he, while singing, would become overwhelmed with admiration for his brother, that he would look from him to me with half-open eyes and pantomime with a soft gesture of the hand, as if saying, "*He* did it. Isn't it wonderful? Isn't *he* wonderful?". . . I shall never forget that evening – the enthusiasm of the two brothers about the music, their anxiety to do it justice, their joy at its being appreciated and with it all their touching devotion for each other.'

With the production team in place – the Theatre Guild hired

Serge Soudekeine as set designer, Alexander Smallens (who had been the conductor for Virgil Thomson's all-Negro opera *Four Saints in Three Acts* although for some bizarre reason, Thomson was furious at this choice) as musical director, and Alexander Steinert as vocal coach – it was casting time. George and DuBose had always envisaged *Porgy and Bess* with an all-black cast and trained black opera singers were a rare breed in 1935. But they did exist. The critic Olin Downes had spoken with George about Todd Duncan, a baritone who taught music at Howard University in Washington DC and who had quite a reputation among the cognoscenti for recitals and concert performances, including the one Downes had heard, an all-black production of *Cavalleria Rusticana*. As soon as it became clear that Paul Robeson was not available, Duncan was invited to New York to sing for George. He arrived with a selection of arias but without an accompanist. George accompanied him, ('Imagine a Negro, auditioning for a Jew, singing an old Italian aria', Duncan said later) and wouldn't even allow him to finish before he interrupted him to ask: *Will you be my Porgy?*

The voice was perfect – rich, full, and flexible – and George wanted him badly, but his lack of stage experience worried the Theatre Guild producers who were, after all, staking a huge production on him. George invited him back to sing for them, paying his train fare and that of his wife, and he was promptly engaged.

Bess, in the person of a voice student, Anne Brown, arrived at the apartment one day with

Todd Duncan and Anne Brown

no experience at all, having been told by one of her Juilliard teachers that Mr Gershwin was approachable. She asked to sing for him and was hired on the spot. The other major roles were taken by experienced and well-trained performers who had spent their professional lives trying to be taken seriously as opera singers and whose major problem with *Porgy and Bess* was that George wanted it performed in the vernacular, complete with the peculiarities of speech and singing that he had heard with Heyward in South Carolina. It must have been a sight to see when this New York Jew got up on stage during rehearsals with 65 black singers to demonstrate to them how to be more Negro.

The role of Sportin' Life, the drug dealer and catalyst for Bess's defection, presented different difficulties. The dancer John Bubbles couldn't read music, was undisciplined, unprofessional and a nightmare throughout rehearsals. In order to get him to learn how to sing his big first act number, 'It Ain't Necessarily So', the rhythms had to be tap-danced for him. For the formally trained opera singers, he was the Sportin' Life from hell. According to an exasperated Todd Duncan, he 'would hold a particular note two beats on Monday night but on Tuesday night he might sustain that same note through six beats', so they never knew what he was going to do and they were convinced that this uncertainty adversely affected their own performances.

It has often been pointed out that not a single member of the production or creative team of *Porgy and Bess* was black. True, but in the 1930s it would have been astonishing if there was even one black backstage professional with the experience to carry such a big show. Even at the time, a number of black luminaries attacked *Porgy and Bess* on just these grounds, some without even hearing the work themselves. No less a composer than Duke Ellington, whose own black folk opera remained unfinished at his death, commented furiously: 'no Negro could possibly be fooled by *Porgy and Bess*'. And the black journalist, Ralph Meadows,

THE THEATRE GUILD presents

PORGY and BESS

MUSIC BY

GEORGE GERSHWIN

LIBRETTO BY

DuBOSE HEYWARD

LYRICS BY

DuBOSE HEYWARD and IRA GERSHWIN

PRODUCTION DIRECTED BY
ROUBEN MAMOULIAN

GERSHWIN PUBLISHING CO.
RKO BLDG. NEW YORK N.
CHAPPELL & CO. INC.
SOLE SELLING AGENT
MADE IN U.S.A.

claimed that even the choral and ensembles 'have a conservatory twang', meaning that the opera (which he called 'a musical hybrid') was a classical musician's idea of the Negro but not, in fact, properly Negro at all.

Rehearsals, with the exception of the chaos caused by Bubbles' shenanigans, were calm and tightly under the control of the experienced Mamoulian. George sat quietly in the back row, eating peanuts, until there was a question about the score. His pride and his joy in his music could have been mistaken for conceit in any other man, but in Gershwin it was simply that he could not believe that he had written such marvellous music and he didn't hesitate to say so. 'He praised his creations without any self-consciousness or false modesty,' Mamoulian said. 'Conceit is made of much sterner stuff – it was not that with George.'

Four days before *Porgy and Bess* opened in Boston on 30 September 1935, George Gershwin turned 37. His opera was a triumph. Bubbles' performance was word-perfect, note-accurate, and his dancing raised the roof. His performance was mercurial and dazzling, the definition of star quality. Todd Duncan and Anne Brown were in fine voice and became the passionate couple they had never been in rehearsal. The choruses soared. The cast members were singing for their race as well as their livelihoods. This, they seemed to be saying that night, this is what we can do when we're allowed the tools and the opportunity. The opening night audience stood and roared its approval. The critics were lavish in their praise. It was, they agreed, the crowning achievement of Gershwin's life so far.

It ain't necessarily so

'Very few composers, if any, would have stood by and witnessed with comparative calm the dismemberment of their brain-child.'

ALEXANDER STEINERT ON THE CUTS TO PORGY AND BESS

The triumphant opening night in Boston was not without its downside. After the cheers had died down, George went for a walk on Boston Common with Mamoulian, the vocal coach Alexander Steinert, who had wrought such miracles with the choral singing, and Kay Swift. Under discussion was the strongly held view of the Theatre Guild producers, and even Mamoulian, that *Porgy and Bess* was, at just over three hours running time, too long for Broadway.

During that walk in the park, George participated in the butchering of his pride and joy. From his lovingly crafted folk opera he allowed cuts amounting to a quarter of the total score. Even Steinert was amazed that George was so philosophical but he was forgetting that George was a highly experienced Broadway composer, a man accustomed to cuts and adjustments, not a precious concert-maker whose every note was indispensable. Steinert was also reckoning without George's insecurity, the legacy of his unorthodox and incomplete education. Lacking exam results, he needed the validation that came with knowing that others agreed with him or, in this case, that he agreed with those who he believed could make *Porgy and Bess* a success on Broadway.

To fail there with the most important work he had ever created, the one that was his passport to immortality, would have

'One utterance may be recorded which came from the heart of the man and is illustrative of his stature. It came at the crossroads of his career, long after his dissatisfaction with Broadway musical comedy; even after he had unfolded his pinions and lifted himself into the realm of serious music: *Do you think*, he asked with naïveté, *that now I am capable of grand operas? Because, you know*, he continued, *all I've got is a lot of talent and plenty of chutzpah.*'

JEROME KERN

been unbearable. That is why he listened to those who asked him to cut his masterpiece and that is why the show that opened at the Alvin Theatre on 10 October 1935, lacked the fluency and operatic sweep that had caused such a sensation in Boston less than two weeks earlier.

It also lacked several songs and the opening 'Jazzbo Brown' piano music that had set the scene for 'Summertime' which now opened the opera cold (except for 20 salvaged bars preceding it). With the exception of the removal of 'Buzzard Song', which was a relief to Todd Duncan as until then he had had three big songs back to back in Act Two, every excision has, with the benefit of history and several subsequent productions of the full score, been proven to be a mistake.

The audience received the truncated show with enthusiasm but the critics were decidedly mixed. Several critics, including longtime fan Olin Downes, had doubts about Gershwin's operatic technique and many thought there was too much Broadway, too many 'song hits' in the score for it to be successful on its own terms as a grand opera. Most vitriolic, indeed personally insulting, was the composer Virgil Thomson. A fine music writer, he was famously waspish and iconoclastic, not to mention egocentric. Worse, he had himself, with Gertrude Stein, written an opera for an all-black cast, the incomprehensible *Four Saints in Three Acts.*

Thomson mixed a discussion of the technical aspects of composing with derogatory comments about the musical content itself, generously interspersed with some of the most anti-Semitic slurs ever printed in a non-Fascist 'respectable' paper: 'I do not like fake folklore, nor fidgety accompaniments, nor bittersweet harmony nor six-part choruses, nor gefilte fish orchestration . . . At best it is a . . . highly unsavory stirring-up of Israel, Africa and the Gaelic Isles . . . Gershwin does not even know what an opera is.'

George was wounded to the quick. While George was confident of the quality of *Porgy and Bess,* he was hurt enough to try to answer the critics (rarely a good idea except later for biographers) in the *New York Times: . . . I am not ashamed of writing songs at any time so long as they are good songs . . . Nearly all of Verdi's operas contain what are known as "song hits".* Carmen *is almost a collection of song hits . . . I have used sustained symphonic music to unify entire scenes and I prepared myself for that task by further study in counterpoint and modern harmony.* His friend, Ann Ronell, who had given him the *Carmen* analogy, said that he remained very hurt, the first time any of his friends had seen him so depressed.

To say that history has vindicated him is to underestimate the value of *Porgy and Bess.* Gershwin (and, of course, Heyward, and to a lesser extent, Ira) did no less than define the American musical theatre of the 20th century with this work. Whether it is a 'show' or a musical or an operetta or a folk opera or a grand opera matters not a jot. With the cuts restored, it has been produced in opera houses, theatres, and school gymnasia all over the world and its insights into American decency, honour, and humanity have enlightened audiences from Australia to Zimbabwe.

One of my most cherished memories is seeing a sophisticated Milanese audience at La Scala (where they traditionally hate everything that isn't Italian and 19th century) on their feet cheering an all-black American cast from the Houston Grand Opera for nearly half an hour. Another was the opening night of *Porgy and Bess* at Glyndebourne where the audience was stunned into silence by the beauty of the then-new Trevor Nunn production starring Willard White and Cynthia Haymon.

If George Gershwin had written nothing but *Porgy and Bess* – no 'Embraceable You', no *Rhapsody in Blue,* no 'I Got Rhythm', no *Concerto in F* – his place in history would be assured. But it closed after 124 performances and lost about $70,000, an enormous amount of money at that time. George's share of the box office receipts wasn't enough to cover the cost of copying the score.

Shall We Dance? · 1935 - 1937

I have more tunes in my head than I could write down in a hundred years.

GEORGE GERSHWIN

Suddenly, after 20 intensive months of work on *Porgy and Bess,* George had no immediate project to occupy himself. He went on vacation to Mexico with his psychiatrist Gregory Zilboorg (who seems at this distance more than a little 'psycho' himself) and his friend, Edward Warburg, Kay Swift's cousin by marriage. It was not a success. Zilboorg, introduced to him by Kay Swift, who was seeing him at the time ('a mistake', she subsequently admitted), was a control freak who specialised in making his celebrity patients uncomfortable. A considerable linguist, he spent most of the Mexican adventure speaking Spanish, thereby, apparently deliberately, excluding George who couldn't wait to return to New York.

Once back, there were concerts (two more all-Gershwins at Lewisohn Stadium) and George made a stunning *Porgy and Bess* orchestral suite, distilling the shape and substance into a piece for the concert hall. Much later Ira renamed it *Catfish Row* because by that time (1942) George's own *Suite* had fallen into disuse and conductor Fritz Reiner had commissioned another, *A Symphonic Picture of Porgy and Bess,* from Robert Russell Bennett, which concentrated more on the score's hit songs. In an effort to reduce costs, George also rescored *Porgy* for a smaller orchestra before it started its tour in Philadelphia in January 1936.

The first half of 1936 was spent on the concerts, on an art exhibition in which George exhibited two paintings, and on haggling with the various Hollywood agents and producers who were interested in having both Gershwins go out to Hollywood to work on a variety of film projects. George and Ira expected the bidding for their services to be high and originally demanded $100,000 and a royalty. To their surprise, there was some nervousness about them at the major studios, a conventional fear that, having now written an opera, they would be too highbrow for popular movie musicals. George was first amused, then nonplussed, then furious, when he heard these whispers. He sent a telegram to RKO Studios in August:

. . RUMORS ABOUT HIGHBROW MUSIC RIDICULOUS . . . . AM OUT TO WRITE HITS . . .

RKO relented because they wanted the Gershwins to write a score for Fred Astaire and Ginger Rogers. After much haggling, the agreed fee was $55,000 for 16 weeks' work with an option for a second film at $70'000. Sam Goldwyn at Metro was also in line for a Gershwin score and agreed to wait until their RKO contract would permit. There was nothing to keep them in New York.

The man who helped to define New York as the place to be, supported its architects and interior designers, made Broadway a destination, the arbiter whose taste informed an entire urban society and whose women had set the Big City fashion trends for more than a decade, was off to Los Angeles, barely a town, merely a collection of suburbs with one industry, a mishmash of buildings, and no chic at all.

It was the end of an era, the end of a certain kind of life, for New York and for George and for his friends, including the woman who, by now divorced and free to marry George, was somehow never asked – Kay Swift. Years later in 1987, when asked why she had divorced James Warburg, she told Joan Peyser: 'I had a happy career, was fond of my husband, had three children.

Everything seemed all right. But I didn't like being in love with somebody else while I was married.'

We don't know whether there was an ultimatum, or a test of their strength as a couple or just a parting of the ways in recognition that there was no future to the relationship. But what is known is that when Kay waved goodbye to George at Newark Airport that August day in 1936 they had agreed not to be in contact at all for the year that he was planning to be away. She told Edward Jablonski, a close friend, that her husband had agreed to a divorce and said that he would give her a generous income for life, whether or not she re-married, and provide for their daughters, on condition that she would agree not to communicate with George for one year. Although each was aware of the other's activities, they never saw nor spoke to one another again.

In Hollywood again, it was all rather an anti-climax. The brothers were given a sketchy outline of a daft plot in which Fred Astaire was to play a 'Russian' ballet dancer known as Petrov whose name was really Peter P Peters from Pittsburg, PA in love with an American musical comedy star (Ginger Rogers) to be called Linda Keene. They started work, waiting for the full script which, they were assured, would quickly follow.

It seems never to have occurred to any of the Gershwins that they might look for separate accommodation and Lee was dispatched to find a house for them all in Beverly Hills. 1019 North Roxbury Drive, near Sunset, was a spacious house with neighbours such as Jerome Kern, Irving Berlin, and Harold Arlen, old friends from New York, who certainly made the newcomers welcome.

Three months later, there was still no script and their contracted 16 weeks was nearly up. They'd written some songs on spec – 'They All Laughed', 'Let's Call the Whole Thing Off' –

George Gershwin and Irving Berlin

but no scoring was yet possible. However, this was California and the long lazy summer days turned into long lazy autumn days with tennis, swimming, parties, painting, letter writing (he asked after Kay but never contacted her directly), happily filling the time until work finally intervened in the shape of a halfway usable script. Then, of course, it got frantic, just like Broadway, keeping pace with the shooting, writing songs overnight, staying up all hours round the piano at their house on Roxbury Drive, and then unwinding by playing 'til all hours at someone else's house. Soon what he was playing was 'They Can't Take That Away From Me', now a Gershwin standard, from their movie score full of classic songs.

By late October, the movie had been retitled *Shall We Dance* with a cheerful title song. What caused the most trouble was the final sequence, a ballet supposed to be reminiscent of *An American in Paris.* It went through so many incarnations – from Latin to jazz to pop to classical – that sweet-tempered and accommodating George walked out one day saying he'd be happy to write whatever the studio wanted as a finale, if only someone would *tell* him what they wanted. Eventually, of course, the finale transmuted into a fine piece of Gershwinesque scoring, culminating in a medley of the movie's best songs. The best piece of orchestral music in the movie, though, has to be 'Walking the Dog', a little masterpiece.

George watched the filming closely, interested in the process and intrigued by how many people had a finger in the movie pie: *It fascinates me to see the amazing things they do with sound recording,* he reported to Mabel Schirmer. *And lighting. And cutting. And so forth.* Apart from that, he was bored and lonely. He didn't much care for the way his songs were used in the film and, in this regard, he had far less influence in Hollywood than on Broadway. Also, he hadn't found a regular girlfriend, although he was seeing Simone Simon as well as a number of other Hollywood starlets. As he wrote to Mabel, he felt that *the girls (out here) are surprisingly selfish, stupid, and career conscious. Have you seen Kay?* he asked her in every letter.

He briefly thought of returning to New York for a couple of weeks around Christmastime *but I don't see where I can find the time . . . Please tell me some news about . . . the town.* The journey to New York from Los Angeles was long and neither George nor Ira could go far afield during shooting in case there was a crisis that required a new song or the adjustment of an existing one, and George was busy with a concert tour of the West Coast, and so the family – Rose and the Godowskys – came to them instead. Throughout January and February, George continued to play concerts in San Francisco, Seattle, and Los Angeles, and which always sold out to attentive, enthusiastic audiences.

As soon as their work on *Shall We Dance* was finished, in the middle of March 1937, RKO exercised their option for another Astaire-Rogers vehicle. As it turned out, what became *A Damsel in Distress,* would indeed star Astaire but without Rogers. Instead, Joan Fontaine was drafted in as co-star. This time, though, George was used to the lack of respect accorded composers in Hollywood and determined not to expend undue energy on what he considered a secondary art to the Broadway musical so, although he and Ira wrote the songs, the incidental music and underscoring was contracted out, usually to the reliable Robert Russell Bennett.

But Not For Me · 1937

'You only made one mistake, George. You died.' GEORGE S KAUFMAN

With the benefit of hindsight, it is possible to see the pattern of events that, taken collectively, might have signalled George's mortal illness had they been seen and understood by a qualified observer. At the time, though, they seemed unrelated, a series of minor inconveniences from which he quickly recovered. The 'composer's stomach' that he had suffered from all his life was part of his hypochondria, a joke to his friends. Hypochondriacs have a hard time when they complain about their health. Sometimes, though, they really are ill.

As far back as 1934, when George was on his 28-city, 28-concert, 28-day tour, Mitch Miller, who had played in the orchestra, told Joan Peyser that George, getting off a train, complained of the smell of burning garbage. Said Miller, then aged 23: 'I remember thinking that was funny because neither I nor anybody else smelled it.' In November 1936, George had several bouts of dizziness which were either witnessed by or mentioned to various friends but they took no more notice of them than he did.

Now, in February 1937, while playing a concert in Los Angeles, he had a most unusual (for him) lapse of memory in the *Concerto in F*. It wasn't a disaster, he didn't have to stop, but he missed some notes and seemed to a knowledgeable concertgoer briefly disorientated. At the same time, he said later, he felt dizzy and could smell burning rubber. But he had a thorough medical examination that week and was given a clean bill of health.

Jerome Kern, Dorothy Fields and George Gershwin and the Ambassador Hotel in Los Angeles in 1937

By the end of March, he and Ira were well into the score for *A Damsel in Distress*. The script was by his old friend, Plum Wodehouse. *Damsel* paired Joan Fontaine (who could neither sing nor dance) with Fred Astaire. One of the few advantages of this odd choice was that the repertory company customarily assembled for a Rogers-Astaire movie was on this occasion replaced by an extremely talented cast, including the comic geniuses, George Burns and Gracie Allen, in supporting roles. Despite having to write for a non-singer, George was enjoying *Damsel* more than he had *Shall We Dance* and had written eight songs for the film including 'Nice Work If You Can Get It' and one of the true classics, 'A Foggy Day'.

Ira wrote in his memoirs: 'About 1am George returned from a party, full of life, took off his dinner jacket, sat down at the piano and said, "How about some work? Got any ideas?"' They decided to fill the hole in the picture where Astaire wanders in the grounds of a castle and they wrote 'A Foggy Day', faster than any song ever before. 'We finished the refrain, words and music, in less than an hour . . . Next day the song still sounded good so we started on the verse (which took two days).' The film's director, George Stevens, did them proud, making the most of their beautiful song by surrounding Fred with the best special effects fog that money could then buy.

As soon as *Damsel* was finished, George and Ira started work, as promised, on *The Goldwyn Follies* for Sam Goldwyn. George was still pursuing an active social life, falling briefly in love with various actresses and less briefly with Paulette Goddard (who was then married to Charlie Chaplin), at his usual round of dinners and celebrity parties where he was inevitably the entertainment as well as the prize guest.

Working for Sam Goldwyn was no fun. After George and Ira had more or less completed the songs, Goldwyn sent for them as though they were house musicians, to play them in his office for a 'jury' of his yes-men. George was furious; surely, he thought, he was far too distinguished to be auditioning songs as in his early days at Remick's?

He wasn't feeling well, complaining more frequently of headaches and dizziness. Even he put it down to overwork and the stress (a word they didn't use then) of working for Goldwyn: *It's too bad our contracts followed each other so closely as we could both use a month's rest,* he wrote to Mabel. *Anyway, the silver lining is that after* The Goldwyn Follies *we are going to take a long vacation.* New York and Kay were on his mind, also possibly a concert tour in Europe.

Lee Gershwin dismissed George's headaches, and confided to friends that he was just bidding for attention. She told him to his face that he was imagining this new malady just as he had

Gershwin's last love affair was with the actress Paulette Goddard, seen here dancing with her husband Charlie Chaplin in 1940

imagined so many previous illnesses. It is not surprising that she didn't take seriously what, in retrospect, was as serious as it is possible to be.

The Goldwyn Follies was a shambles. Sam Goldwyn had hired comics, opera singers and ballet dancers (with George Balanchine as choreographer). All that was missing was a *bona fide* movie star or any actors who might have held the film together. The Gershwins' songs were either not used well or not used at all. Sometimes they were sung under dialogue scenes, and although George and Ira started 'Our Love Is Here To Stay', it became clear that there was no room for the whole song in the movie. There was therefore no point in their completing the verse. Only later did Ira and Oscar Levant remember what George had sketched at the piano for the verse and finish it.

By June, George was in a very bad mood, unusually for him, snapping and throwing tantrums, and complaining of fatigue and headaches to the point where even Lee suggested a full physical examination. On 9 June he once again got a clean bill of health from several doctors, who had examined him at home.

Some of his wide circle of acquaintances, including his faithful driver and assistant, Paul Mueller, suggested that the headaches might have been caused by a metal contraption he'd been using to stimulate growth of his thinning hair. In any case, everyone in Hollywood agreed that working for Goldwyn was enough to give anyone a headache.

His affair with Paulette Goddard continued behind Charlie Chaplin's back and although he was, from his letters to Mabel Schirmer, besotted with her, he knew in a contest between Chaplin and Gershwin there would be no choice to be made. Perhaps that was part of the attraction: he had no need to make a commitment to her because she was married already. In New York there was still Kay Swift, working now as staff composer for Radio City Music Hall, the woman with whom he had most in common, who was the closest he ever came to a soulmate, the one he relied on for professional and personal comfort. And there was no shortage of Hollywood babes, starlets and genuine stars, in a town full of girls whose only job was to look beautiful.

George, despite the evidence of many conversations and letters that spring about his desire to marry and his endless speculation with his close friends Mabel Schirmer, George Pallay, Oscar Levant and others about whom he should choose, never got even close. Harold Arlen told him he simply wasn't the type to marry and would always 'play the field'. Edward Jablonski says that this obvious truth angered George and he dropped the subject. For some reason he wanted his friends to believe that his intentions were honourable, that he intended to marry just as soon as he found, or chose, the right woman.

The headaches, described by one physician as 'severe, pounding, got worse and George became abnormally sensitive to light. His mood changes were now obvious even to those from whom he tried to hide them such as Paulette, who was so alarmed by his distraction after lunching with him on 22 June that she persuaded him to check himself into hospital. At Cedars of Lebanon hospital they put him through a very thorough battery of tests – blood, x-rays, eyes, heart and neurological. When they released him on 26 June, the diagnosis was 'most likely hysteria'. The best hospital in Los Angeles could find nothing physically or organically wrong with him.

If not physical, then logic dictated that a psychiatrist should be brought in to fix the neurosis that was causing the physical symptoms. The famous psychoanalyst chosen, Dr Ernest Simmel, was himself convinced that George's illness was, in fact, organic.

His symptoms were now so severe that they rendered George non-functional for part of every day, but he went on with his regular life to the extent that his illness permitted, working with Ira, giving concerts, going to parties, and squiring girls around

Hollywood. Every day the headaches and light-sensitivity became worse. His sister-in-law was, once physical causes had been eliminated, less than sympathetic. Seeing George fall when leaving a restaurant, she snapped: 'Just leave him there, all he wants is attention.' Another time, when his physical coordination was failing, and he was spilling things, she asked him to leave the dinner table. Ira had to help George to his room and the brothers caught each other's eyes. 'I'll never forget that look as long as I live,' wrote Ira later.

The tension between George and Lee was such that George, his nurse, Paul Levy, and his assistant, Paul Mueller, moved into Yip Harburg's neighbouring house but not before his old friend S N Behrman came to see him, on 3 July, with Harold Arlen and another friend. 'He was very pale,' Behrman recalled. 'The light had gone from his eyes. He seemed old . . . the spring had gone out of his walk.' It was clear to Behrman that this was no 'nervous disorder'. After only a few minutes, George asked to be taken back to his room.

On the evening of Friday 9 July, George's eyes 'seemed to swell' and he fell unconscious before being admitted to Cedars of Lebanon. Only now, it seems, when George was already in a coma, did any of the doctors take seriously the possibility that he had a brain tumour. They did a spinal tap, which reduced the pressure on his brain somewhat, and began to talk seriously about brain surgery.

The Gershwin juggernaut swung into action. The White House was called to locate and retrieve Dr Walter Dandy, the best neurosurgeon in the United States, who was then sailing in the Chesapeake Bay with the Governor of Maryland. The President's staff enlisted the US Navy to send a message to the yacht and then a Coast Guard cutter to pick Dandy up and fly him to Los Angeles. He was then to be flown in a chartered plane to Newark, where he would board a flight to Los Angeles.

Speaking to the Cedars medical team by ship-to-shore radio he concurred that surgery should take place as soon as possible. In the meantime, Dr Carl Rand, the top neurosurgeon at Cedars of Lebanon, had located another distinguished neurosurgeon, Dr Howard C Naffziger. He was on holiday also, but closer to hand, in Lake Tahoe. He was soon in Los Angeles, examined George at 9pm, and recommended immediate surgery. The operation began just after midnight on Saturday with Rand as lead surgeon and Naffziger as consultant.

The operating theatre was full; there were about 20 doctors and nurses in attendance. They found what had eluded all the tests: first a cyst, then, below it, a tumour in the right temporal lobe, embedded deeply in the brain. Neither the cyst nor the tumour had shown up on X-rays and, of course, there were no CT scans or MRIs to check the diagnosis or even steroids to reduce the swelling. Even if there had been, and even if George's illness had been treated as physical from the beginning, this was a form of brain cancer, glioblastoma, which is to this day too virulent and fast growing to have been treated, except possibly temporarily.

The extended family – Ira, Lee, Henry Botkin, Oscar Levant, the Paleys and several others – collected in a visitors' room on the hospital's fourth floor, while George Pallay appointed himself liaison for the family by positioning himself at a desk with a telephone just outside the operating theatre. For the entire five hours of surgery he remained at his post, giving the waiting relatives and friends regular bulletins whenever a nurse or a doctor came out of the theatre.

Once the tumour had been discovered, there really was no hope. George was taken back to his room at about seven and at exactly 10.35 on Sunday morning 11 July 1937, George Gershwin died, never having regained consciousness since he slipped into a coma on Friday night.

He was two months short of his 39th birthday.

They Can't Take That Away From Me

'He was a lucky young man
Lucky to be so in love with the world And lucky because the
world was so in love with him'

OSCAR HAMMERSTEIN II, AT THE MEMORIAL CONCERT FOR

GEORGE GERSHWIN, 8 SEPTEMBER 1937

The funeral was at Temple Emanu-el on Fifth Avenue in New York, on 15 July. It rained. There was a simultaneous service in Los Angeles at the B'nai B'rith Temple. The music was sombre and the atmosphere one of understandable shock. George had left no instructions for the conduct or content of his funeral. If he had, surely there would have been at least one, possibly many, Gershwin compositions played that day.

But George left no will. He was a young man still, thinking about marriage and children, full of plans for a new opera with DuBose Heyward and enthusiastic about some sketches he had made for a String Quartet. Someone would find something to get rid of the headaches and he'd take his long planned holiday break to New York, and to Europe. He'd get together with Mabel Schirmer and Kay Swift. His life was in front of him.

George Gershwin 1937

Dying suddenly, intestate, and rich (George left nearly half a million dollars, a huge fortune in 1937), it was inevitable that there would be claimants, legitimate and otherwise, and that the family would want to protect themselves. Rose was the sole beneficiary and Ira later applied for judicial adjudication on the division of their work. No one was prepared, or could have been prepared, for the accident of biology that was to kill George Gershwin so young.

Kill George Gershwin? No, not that. In my ears ring the applause of that La Scala crowd in Milan for *Porgy and Bess; Rhapsody in Blue* assails me when I try to book an airline ticket; a pianist friend (Jeffrey Siegel) deconstructs a *Prelude* and then plays it with consummate skill and delicacy; a soprano reduces me to tears with an *a cappella* version of 'Summertime'; a piano roll reproduces George's quirky phrasing; a child with a mouth-organ murders 'Swanee'. These are not memories, not really. These are living embodiments of George Gershwin with all the gifts he gave us.

And then I look at that scrap of newsreel, at the rehearsal footage of the smiling, sexy, young man with the pretty girl dancers, striking up his own band, designing his own city, making his own world, and leaving it to us.

Kill George Gershwin?

Never.

Long Live Jazz!!!!

George Gershwin.

Chronology

Year	Age	Life
1895		Marriage of Rose Bruskin and Morris Gershovitz, recently arrived in New York from St Petersburg. Rose is 19, Morris 24. They live in New York's Lower East Side.
1896		6 December: Birth of Rose and Morris's first child, Israel, also known as Isadore, Izzy or Ira. Family moves house frequently.
1898		26 September: Birth of Jacob Gershwine, later George, in Brooklyn.
1900	2	14 March: Birth of Arthur Gershwine.
1906	8	6 December: Birth of Frances Gershwine.
1908	10	Meets young violinist Maxie Rosenzweig, later virtuoso Max Rosen.
1909	11	George begins to learn piano. Rose buys George a piano
1912	14	Begins to study piano with Charles Hambitzer.

Year	History	Culture
1895	Lumière brothers invent the cinematograph. Guglielmo Marconi invents wireless telegraphy. Wilhelm Röntgen discovers X-rays.	H G Wells, *The Time Machine.* W B Yeats, *Poems.* Wilde, *The Importance of Being Earnest.*
1896	Theodore Herzl articulates Zionism. First Olympic Games of the modern era held in Athens. Antoine (Henri) Becquerel discovers radioactivity of uranium.	Giacomo Puccini, *La Bohème.* Thomas Hardy, *Jude the Obscure.*
1898	Spanish-American War: Spain loses Cuba, Puerto Rico and the Philippines. Britain conquers Sudan.	Joseph Conrad, *The Nigger of the Narcissus.* Strindberg, *Inferno.* Edmond Rostand, *Cyrano de Bergerac.*
1900	In China, Boxer Rebellion (until 1901). Aspirin introduced. First Zeppelin flight.	Puccini, *Tosca.* Conrad, *Lord Jim.* Sigmund Freud, *The Interpretation of Dreams*
1906	Duma created in Russia. Revolution in Iran.	Henri Matisse, *Bonheur de vivre.* Maxim Gorky, *The Mother* (until 1907).
1908	Bulgaria becomes independent. Austria-Hungary annexes Bosnia-Herzegovina.	Gustav Mahler, *Das Lied von der Erde* (until 1909). E M Forster, *A Room with a View.*
1909	In Turkey, Young Turk revolution. Henry Ford introduces Model T car.	Strauss, *Elektra.* Rabindranath Tagore, *Gitanjali.* Sergey Diaghilev forms Les Ballets Russes. F T Marinetto publishes manifesto of futurism in *Le Figaro.*
1912	Titanic sinks. Dr Sun Yat-sen establishes Republic of China. Stainless steel invented.	Arnold Schoenberg, *Pierrot lunaire.* Carl Jung, *The Psychology of the Unconscious.*

Year	Age	Life
1913	15	Enters the High School of Commerce. Summer: George's first musical engagement as relief pianist at the Catskills holiday resort.
1914	16	May: George leaves the High School of Commerce to take up job as a pianist on Tin Pan Alley for Remick's.
1915	17	Begins recording piano rolls. Writes first song, 'Since I Lost You'. Meets young Fred Astaire.
1916	18	First published song, 'When You Want 'Em, You Can't Get 'Em; When You've Got 'Em, You Don't Want 'Em'. First song in musical theatre, 'Making of a Girl' in *The Passing Show of 1916.*
1917	19	First published instrumental piece, *Rialto Ripples,* a piano rag solo. Quits job at Remick's. Meets Jerome Kern while working as rehearsal pianist on his *Miss 1917.*
1918	20	Signs publishing contract with Max Dreyfus for his songs. George 'interpolates' songs in several Broadway shows. October: 'The Real American Folksong (is a Rag)' – first song with Ira Gershwin used in a musical, *Ladies First.*
1919	21	May: First full-scale musical, *La-La Lucille,* opens on Broadway. Composes 'Swanee'.
1920	22	June: Provides score for *George White's Scandals of 1920.*
1921	23	Writes songs for the *Scandals* and enrols at Columbia University Music Department to take summer courses in orchestration and 19th century Romanticism in Music. In the autumn he meets Kay Swift.

Year	History	Culture
1913	In US, Woodrow Wilson becomes president (until 1921). Hans Geiger invents Geiger counter.	Stravinsky, *The Rite of Spring.* Guillaume Apollinaire, *Les peintres cubistes.* D H Lawrence, *Sons and Lovers.* Marcel Proust, *A la recherche du temps perdu* (until 1927).
1914	28 June: Archduke Franz Ferdinand assassinated in Sarajevo. World War One begins. Panama Canal opens.	James Joyce, *Dubliners.* Ezra Pound, *Des Imagistes.*
1915	Dardanelles/Gallipoli campaign (until 1916). In US, William J Simmons revives the Ku Klux Klan. Albert Einstein publishes general theory of relativity.	John Buchan, *The Thirty-Nine Steps.* D H Lawrence, *The Rainbow.* Marcel Duchamp, *The Large Glass.* Pablo Picasso, *Harlequin.*
1916	Battle of Somme. Battle of Jutland. Easter Rising in Ireland. Arabs revolt against Ottoman Turks.	Guillaume Apollinaire, *Le poète assassiné.* G B Shaw, *Pygmalion.* Dada movement launched in Zurich with Cabaret Voltaire.
1917	In Russia, Tsar Nicholas II abdicates: Communists seize power under Vladimir Lenin. US enters World War One. Balfour Declaration on Palestine: Britain favours creation of Jewish state without prejudice to non-Jewish communities.	First recording of New Orleans jazz. Franz Kafka, *Metamorphosis.* T S Eliot, *Prufrock and Other Observations.* Giorgio de Chirico, *Le Grand Métaphysique.*
1918	In Russia, Tsar Nicholas II and family executed. 11 November: Armistice agreement ends First World War. 'Spanish flu' epidemic kills at least 20m people in Europe, US and India.	Oswald Spengler, *The Decline of the West,* Volume 1. Amédée Ozenfant and Le Corbusier, *Après le Cubisme.* Paul Klee, *Gartenplan.*
1919	In US, Prohibition begins. Irish Civil War (until 1921).	United Artists formed with Charlie Chaplin, Mary Pickford, Douglas Fairbanks and D W Griffith as partners.
1920	IRA formed. First meeting of League of Nations.	
1921	Washington Treaty signed: US, Britain, France, and Japan agree to respects each other's position in the Pacific.	Sergey Prokofiev, *The Love of Three Oranges.* Luigi Pirandello, *Six Characters in Search of an Author.* Chaplin, *The Kid.*

Year	Age	Life
1922	24	August: Composes *Blue Monday* for *George White's Scandals of 1922.*
1923	25	April: *The Rainbow* opens in London. 1 November: First concert accompanying Eva Gauthier at the Aeolian Hall, New York.
1924	26	21 January: *Sweet Little Devil* opens in New York. 12 February: Paul Whiteman's concert 'An Experiment in Modern Music'. George plays piano for the premiere of *Rhapsody in Blue.* Records an abridged version in June. 11 September: *Primrose* opens at the Winter Garden, London. 1 December: *Lady, Be Good!* opens at Liberty Theatre, New York.
1925	27	April: *Tell Me More* has a brief run in New York. Is much more successful in London in May. July: Becomes first American composer to be on cover of *Time* magazine. 3 December: Premiere of *Concerto in F,* at Carnegie Hall. *Tip-Toes* and *Song of the Flame* open in New York at end of December; both are successful.
1926	28	14 April: *Lady, Be Good!,* starring Fred and Adele Astaire, opens in London. September: Reads *Porgy* and is immediately enthused. 8 November: *Oh, Kay!* opens in New York.
1927	29	21 April: First electrical recording of *Rhapsody in Blue,* with the Paul Whiteman Orchestra. Fierce row with Whiteman over tempi. 25 April: First attempt at a watercolour. 5 September: *Strike Up the Band* opens in Philadelphia but closes rapidly. 22 November: *Funny Face* opens in New York.
1928	30	10 January: *Rosalie* opens in New York. 7 March: Meets Ravel at a party. March to June: Gershwins in London, Paris, Berlin, Vienna. Collects inspiration for *An American in Paris;* meets Prokofiev, Kurt Weill, Franz Lehár and Berg. 1 August: completes two piano version of *An American in Paris;* premieres at Carnegie Hall on 13 December.
1929	31	2 July: *Show Girl* opens in New York.
1930	32	14 January: *Strike Up the Band* (revised version) opens in New York. 14 October: *Girl Crazy* opens in New York. A great success. 1 November: Frankie Gershwin marries Leopold Godowsky II 5 November: George, Ira and Leonore (Lee) head for Hollywood.

Year	History	Culture
1922	Soviet Union formed. Benito Mussolini's fascists march on Rome.	T S Eliot, *The Waste Land.* Joyce, *Ulysses.*
1923	Ottoman empire ends; Palestine, Transjordan and Iraq to Britain; Syria to France.	Le Corbusier, *Vers une architecture.*
1924	Vladimir Lenin dies. Greece is proclaimed a republic. Rioting between Hindus and Muslims in Delhi. Calvin Coolidge wins US presidential elections.	Forster, *A Passage to India.* Thomas Mann, *The Magic Mountain.* André Breton, first surrealist manifesto.
1925	Pact of Locarno, multilateral treaty intended to guarantee peace in Europe. Chiang Kai-shek launches campaign to unify China. Discovery of ionosphere.	Erik Satie dies. F Scott Fitzgerald, *The Great Gatsby.* Kafka, *The Trial.* Sergey Eisenstein, *Battleship Potemkin.* Television invented.
1926	Germany joins League of Nations. France establishes Republic of Lebanon. Hirohito becomes emperor of Japan.	Puccini, *Turandot.* T E Lawrence, *The Seven Pillars of Wisdom.* A A Milne, *Winnie the Pooh.* Fritz Lang, *Metropolis.*
1927	Joseph Stalin comes to power; Leon Trotsky expelled from Soviet Communist Party. Charles Lindbergh flies across Atlantic.	Martin Heidegger, *Being and Time.* Virginia Woolf, *To the Lighthouse.* BBC public radio launched.
1928	Kellogg-Briand Pact for Peace. Transjordan becomes self-governing under the British mandate. Albania is proclaimed a kingdom. Alexander Fleming discovers penicillin.	Maurice Ravel, *Boléro.* Kurt Weill, *The Threepenny Opera.* Huxley, *Point Counter Point.* D H Lawrence, *Lady Chatterley's Lover.* W B Yeats, *The Tower.* Walt Disney, *Steamboat Willie.*
1929	Yugoslavia under kings of Serbia. Wall Street Crash.	Ernest Hemingway, *A Farewell to Arms.* Erich Remarque, *All Quiet on the Western Front.* Jean Cocteau, *Les Enfants Terribles.*
1930	Mahatma Gandhi leads Salt March in India. Frank Whittle patents turbojet engine. Pluto discovered.	W H Auden, *Poems.* T S Eliot, 'Ash Wednesday'. William Faulkner, *As I Lay Dying.* Evelyn Waugh, *Vile Bodies.*

Year	Age	Life
1931	33	Work on *Delicious* (film). 19 March: Attends American première of Berg's *Wozzeck*. 26 December: *Of Thee I Sing* opens in New York – a triumph.
1932	34	29 January: Premiere of the *Second Rhapsody* in Boston. 2 May: Publication of *Piano Transcriptions of 18 Songs*. 1 June: Book and lyrics of *Of Thee I Sing* wins a Pulitzer prize.
1933	35	20 January: Unsuccessful run of *Pardon My English*. 22 October: *Let 'Em Eat Cake* opens in New York; poorly received. 26 October : Signs contract for *Porgy*.
1934	36	Working on *Porgy and Bess*. 15 January: Begins national tour of concerts. 19 February to December: Broadcasting of 'Music by Gershwin' radio show.
1935	37	26 August: Rehearsals for *Porgy and Bess* begin in New York. 30 September: Première of *Porgy and Bess* in Boston; opens in New York on 10 October.
1936	38	Work on films and concerts.
1937	39	Begins to experience dizziness and other symptoms. 10-11 February: All-Gershwin concert given by Los Angeles Philharmonic. Work on films, *A Damsel in Distress* and *The Goldwyn Follies*. June: Medical examinations find nothing. 9 July: Slips into a coma. 10 July: Operation to remove a brain tumour. 10.35am 11 July: Gershwin dies.

Year	History	Culture
1931	King Alfonso XIII flees; Spanish republic formed. New Zealand becomes independent. Japan occupies Manchuria. Building of Empire State Building completed in New York.	Antoine de St-Exupéry, *Night Flight*. Rakhmaninov's music is banned in Soviet Union as 'decadent'. Chaplin, *City Lights*. Fritz Lang, *M. Frankenstein* starring Boris Karloff.
1932	Kingdom of Saudi Arabia independent. Kingdom of Iraq independent. James Chadwick discovers neutron. First autobahn opened, between Cologne and Bonn.	Aldous Huxley, *Brave New World*. Jules Romains, *Les hommes de bonne volonté*. Bertolt Brecht, *The Mother*.
1933	Adolf Hitler appointed German chancellor. F D Roosevelt president in US; launches New Deal.	André Malraux, *La condition humaine*. Gertrude Stein, *The Autobiography of Alice B Toklas*.
1934	In China, Mao embarks on the Long March. Enrico Fermi sets off first controlled nuclear reaction.	Dmitri Shostakovich, *Lady Macbeth of Mtsensk*. Agatha Christie, *Murder on the Orient Express*. Fitzgerald, *Tender is the Night*. Henry Miller, *Tropic of Cancer*.
1935	In Germany, Nuremberg Race Laws enacted. Philippines becomes self-governing. Italy invades Ethiopia.	Christopher Isherwood, *Mr Norris Changes Trains*. Marx Brothers, *A Night at the Opera*.
1936	Edward VIII abdicates throne in Britain; George VI becomes king. Spanish Civil War (until 1939).	Prokofiev, *Peter and the Wolf*. A J Ayer, *Language, Truth and Logic*. BBC public television founded.
1937	Arab-Jewish conflict in Palestine. Japan invades China. Nanjing massacre.	Jean-Paul Sartre, *La Nausée*. John Steinbeck, *Of Mice and Men*. Picasso, *Guernica*.

Major Works

Theatre and Film Works

	Title	Lyrics	Book / Screenplay
1919	La-La-Lucille	B G DeSylva and Arthur Jackson	Frederick Jackson
	Morris Gest Midnight Whirl	B G DeSylva and John Henry Mears	
1920	George White's Scandals of 1920	Arthur Jackson	Andy Rice and George White
1921	A Dangerous Maid	Ira Gershwin (as Arthur Francis)	Charles W Bell
	George White's Scandals of 1921	Arthur Jackson	Arthur 'Bugs' Baer and George White
1922	George White's Scandals of 1922	B G DeSylva and E Ray Goetz	George White and W C Fields
	Blue Monday (Opera A la Afro-American), later reorchestrated as 135th Street	B G DeSylva	B G DeSylva
	Our Nell (with William Daly)	Brian Hooker	A E Thomas and Brian Hooker
1923	The Rainbow	Clifford Grey	Albert de Courville, Edgar Wallace and Noel Scott
	George White's Scandals of 1923	B G DeSylva, E Ray Goetz and Ballard MacDonald	George White and William K Wells
1924	Sweet Little Devil	B G DeSylva	Frank Mandel and Laurence Schwab

	Title	Lyrics	Book / Screenplay
	George White's Scandals of 1924	B G DeSylva	William K Wells and George White
	Primrose	Ira Gershwin and Desmond Carter	Guy Bolton and George Grossmith
	Lady, Be Good!	Ira Gershwin	Guy Bolton and Fred Thompson
1925	Tell Me More	B G DeSylva and Ira Gershwin	Fred Thompson and William K Wells
	Tip-Toes	Ira Gershwin	Guy Bolton and Fred Thompson
	Song of the Flame (with Herbert Stothart)	Otto Harbach and Oscar Hammerstein	Harbach and Hammerstein
1926	Oh, Kay!	Ira Gershwin	Guy Bolton and P G Wodehouse
1927	Strike Up the Band	Ira Gershwin	George S Kaufman
	Funny Face	Ira Gershwin	Fred Thompson and Paul Gerard Smith
1928	Rosalie	P G Wodehouse and Ira Gershwin	William Anthony McGuire and Guy Bolton
1929	Show Girl	Gus Kahn and Ira Gershwin	William Anthony McGuire and J P McEvoy
1930	Strike Up the Band (revised version)	Ira Gershwin	George S Kaufman Morrie Ryskind,
	Girl Crazy	Ira Gershwin Guy Bolton and John McGowan	Guy Bolton and John McGowan
1931	Delicious (film)	Ira Gershwin	Guy Bolton and Sonya Levien
	Of Thee I Sing	Ira Gershwin	George S Kaufman and Morrie Ryskind

	Title	Lyrics	Book / Screenplay
1933	Pardon My English	Ira Gershwin	Herbert Fields
	Let 'Em Eat Cake	Ira Gershwin	George S Kaufman and Morrie Ryskind
1935	Porgy and Bess (opera)	Ira Gershwin and DuBose Heyward	DuBose Heyward, from his novel
	Shall We Dance (film)	Ira Gershwin	Allan Scott and Ernest Pagano
	A Damsel in Distress (film)	Ira Gershwin	P G Wodehouse, Ernest Pagano and S K Lauren
1938	The Goldwyn Follies (film)	Ira Gershwin	Ben Hecht
1946	The Shocking Miss Pilgrim (film)	Ira Gershwin	George Seaton

Concert Works

1924   Rhapsody in Blue
1925   Concerto in F
1926   Preludes for Piano
1928   An American in Paris
1932   Second Rhapsody
        Cuban Overture
        Piano Transcriptions of 18 Songs, also known as George Gershwin's Song-book
1934   Variations on I Got Rhythm

Picture Sources

The author and publishers wish to express their thanks to the following sources of illustrative material and/or permission to reproduce it. They will make proper acknowledgements in future editions in the event that any omissions have occurred.

Akg Images: pp. 121, 134; Corbis: pp. 125; Ed Jablonski/Gershwin Estate: pp 6, 9, 15, 52, 61, 71, 75, 96, 106, 110, 119; Getty Images: pp. 136, 142,147; Lebrecht Music Collection: pp. I iii, 3, 5, 13, 23, 25, 38, 48, 50, 57, 59, 62, 79, 83, 86, 101, 104, 127, 140, 148;Topham Picturepoint: pp. 17, 33, 76, 113.

Selected Songs

(Music by George Gershwin and lyrics by Ira Gershwin unless otherwise noted)

Aren't You Kind of Glad We Did? (The Shocking Miss Pilgrim)

A Woman Is a Sometime Thing (Porgy and Bess)
   Lyrics by DuBose Heyward

The Babbitt and the Bromide (Funny Face)

The Black Bay Polka (The Shocking Miss Pilgrim)

Bess, You Is My Woman Now (Porgy and Bess)
   Lyrics by Ira Gershwin and DuBose Heyward

Bidin' My Time (Girl Crazy)

Boy! What Love Has Done to Me! (Girl Crazy)

But Not for Me (Girl Crazy)

By Strauss (The Show Is On)

Clap Yo' Hands (Oh, Kay!)

Do, Do, Do (Oh, Kay!)

Do It Again (The French Doll)
   Lyrics by B G DeSylva

Embraceable You (Girl Crazy)

Fascinating Rhythm (Lady, Be Good!)

A Foggy Day (A Damsel in Distress)

For You, For Me, For Evermore (The Shocking Miss Pilgrim)

The Half of It, Dearie, Blues (Lady, Be Good!)

How Long Has This Been Going On? (Rosalie)

I Got Plenty o' Nuthin' (Porgy and Bess)
   Lyrics by Ira Gershwin and DuBose Heyward

I Got Rhythm (Girl Crazy)

It Ain't Necessarily So (Porgy and Bess)

I've Got a Crush On You (Treasure Girl)

Let's Call the Whole Thing Off (Shall We Dance)

Looking for a Boy (Tip-Toes)

The Lorelei (Pardon My English)

(Our) Love Is Here to Stay (The Goldwyn Follies)

Love Is Sweeping the Country (Of Thee I Sing)

Love Walked In (The Goldwyn Follies)
(The) Man I Love (deleted from both Lady, Be Good! and Strike Up the Band)
Mine (Let 'Em Eat Cake)
Nice Work If You Can Get It (A Damsel in Distress)
Nobody But You (La-La Lucille)
Of Thee I Sing (Of Thee I Sing)
Oh, Lady Be Good! (Lady, Be Good!)
Sam and Delilah (Girl Crazy)
Shall We Dance (Shall We Dance)
Slap That Bass (Shall We Dance)
So Am I (Lady, Be Good!)
So Are You (Show Girl)
    Lyrics by Ira Gershwin and Gus Kahn
Somebody Loves Me (George White's Scandals of 1924)
   Lyrics by B G DeSylva and Ballard MacDonald
Someone to Watch Over Me (Oh, Kay!)
Soon (Strike Up the Band)
(I'll Build a) Stairway to Paradise (George White's Scandals of 1922)
    Lyrics by Ira Gershwin with B G DeSylva
Strike Up the Band (Strike Up the Band)
Summertime (Porgy and Bess)
   Lyrics by DuBose Heyward
Swanee
   Lyrics by Irving Caesar
Sweet and Low-Down (Tip-Toes)
'S Wonderful (Funny Face)
That Certain Feeling (Tip-Toes)
That Lost Barber Shop Chord (Americana)
There's a Boat Dat's Leavin' Soon for New York (Porgy and Bess)
They All Laughed (Shall We Dance)
They Can't Take That Away From Me (Shall We Dance)
Who Cares? (Shall We Dance)
Wintergreen for President (Of Thee I Sing)

Index

Aalsberg, Henry, 101
Aarons, Alex, 40–1, 56, 58, 90, 114; commences association with Gershwin, 28–9; partnership with Freedley, 62, 67, 75, 82, 109; strained relations with Gershwins, 84; career ends with flop, 116–17
Aarons, Alfred, 28
Aarons, Ella, 56
Actors' Equity, 30
Africa, 28, 122
Allen, Gracie, 140
America, 68–70, 100
American music, 46, 48
Arlen, Harold, 135, 144, 145
Art Deco, 68, 95, 100, 112
Askins, Harry, 25, 121
Astaire, Adele, 17, 41, 56–9, 74–5, 83, 85, 97
Astaire, Fred, 18, 22, 84, 97, 133, 135; partnership with Adele, 17, 41, 56–9, 74–5, 83, 85; first dances with Ginger Rogers, 105; stars with Joan Fontaine, 138, 140
Atkinson, Brooks, 30, 77, 94, 111
Atterbury, Harold, 20

Bach, Johann Sebastian, 87
Balanchine, George, 143
Ballets Russes, 88
Baltimore, 67
Bartók, Béla, 45
Bayes, Nora, 27

Beethoven, Ludwig van, 87
Behrman, S N, 145
Benchley, Robert, 83–4
Bennett, Robert Russell, 132, 138
Berg, Alban, 89–90
Berlin, 69, 89
Berlin, Irving, 19–20, 22, 27, 53, 102, 136; biography, 18; special piano, 18; manages own shows, 109; Gershwin's neighbour, 135; 'Alexander's Ragtime Band', 12, 16, 46
Bernstein, Leonard, 50
Beverly Hills, 107, 135
blue notes, 43–4
blues, 28, 29, 44, 46, 66, 119
Bohm, Adolph, 23
Bolton, Guy, 22, 58, 71, 77, 103, 106
Bordman, Gerald, 29
Bordoni, Irene, 41
Boston, 30–1, 46–8, 78, 98, 111, 117; premiere of *Porgy and Bess,* 128–30; Symphony Hall, 112, 114
Boston Symphony Orchestra, 111–12
Botkin, Henry (Harry), 72, 95, 122, 146
Boulanger, Nadia, 86, 87
Braggiotti, Mario, 88
Brown, Anne, 125–6, 128
Bubbles, John, 126, 128
Buffalo, 78
Burns, George, 10, 140

Caesar, Irving, 19, 24, 30–3
cakewalk, 27, 29
Canada, 79
Caron, Leslie, 92
Carousel, 82
Castle, Irene, 23
Catskill Mountains, 10
Cedars of Lebanon hospital, 144–6
Chaplin, Charlie, 40, 141, 143

Charleston, Mollie, 64
Charleston, SC, 118–20, 122–3
Charleston (dance), 65, 66, 88
Charlot, André, 75
Chasins, Abram 35
Chattauqua, NY, 64
Chotzinoff, Samuel, 67–8
Confrey, Zez, 48
Copland, Aaron, 87, 112
Coward, Noël, 34, 40, 55, 72, 75, 76
Cuba, 114

d'Alvarez, Marguerite, 78
Daly, William, 65, 66, 97, 116
Damrosch, Walter, 54, 63, 65–6, 68, 88, 93, 97
Dandy, Dr Walter, 145
Davies, Marion, 23
Debussy, Claude, 87, 90, 91
DeForrest, Muriel, 32
Depresssion, 111–12, 117
DeSylva, Buddy, 29, 32, 40–2, 46, 47, 56
Diaghilev, Sergei, 88, 90
Dietz, Howard, 76–7
Dillingham, Charles, 23
dogs, 73
Donahue, Lester, 66
Donaldson, Walter, 45
Dorsey, Jimmy, 105
Downes, Olin, 67, 93, 112, 125, 130
Dreyfus, Max, 32–3, 40, 97; Gershwin's publisher, 25–6, 30, 35, 56, 121
Drozdoff, Vladimir, 115
Duke, Vernon, 90
Duncan, Todd, 125, 126, 128, 130
Dvořák, Antonín, 7
Dybbuk, The, 100

Elgar, Edward, 48, 53, 92
Ellington, Duke, 41, 98–9, 126
Elman, Mischa, 54

England, 44
Europe, James, 26
Ewan, David, 55

Fairbanks, Douglas, 30
Farrell, Charles, 107
Fitzgerald, F Scott, 2, 60
Flagler, Harry Harkness, 63
Florida, 79, 95, 106, 123
folk music, 46
Folly Island, 122
Fontaine, Joan, 138, 140
*For Goodness' Sake, Stop
Flirting,* 41, 56
Ford, Helen, 41
Ford, Henry, 24
Foster, Stephen, 31
Francis, Arthur, *see* Gershwin, Ira
Fray, Jacques, 88
Freedley, Vinton, 62, 67,
74–5, 82, 109; strained
relations with Gershwins,
84; introduces Ethel
Merman to Gershwin,
104; career ends with
flop, 116–17
French Doll, The, 41
Friml, Rudolf, 48

Garbo, Greta, 107
Gauguin, Paul, 72
Gauthier, Eva, 45–5, 47,
48, 51, 78, 87, 97
Gaynor, Janet, 107
George Gershwin's Song Book,
114
Georgia Sea Islands, 122
Gershwin, Arthur, 7, 9,
61, 95
Gershwin, Frances (later
Godowsky), 7, 61, 68,
138; dancing, 73; trip to
Europe, 85, 89–90; mar-
riage, 95, 106–7
Gershwin, Morris (origi-
nally Gershovitz), 4–5,
11, 13; uses Gershwine
name, 5; personality and
business ventures, 5–7;
domestic life, 18, 51, 61,

73, 95; and first performance of *Swanee,* 31; and
Frankie's marriage, 106;
death, 114
Gershvin, Rose (originally
Gershovitz, née Bruskin),
4, 138; uses Gershwine
name, 5; personal-
ity and influence, 6, 13,
50, 95; buys piano, 8;
arranges piano lessons,
10; domestic life, 18,
61, 73, 95; and Frankie's
marriage, 106–7; and
Morris's death, 114–15;
beneficiary at George's
death, 147

Gershwin, George: born
Jacob Gershwine, 7; admi-
ration for his brother, 7;
and painting, 2, 7, 72–3,
95–7, 117, 133; interest
in literature, 7, 18; early
interest in music, 7–8, 10;
friendships, 7–8, 13, 18–
19, 24, 40, 60, 64; education, 9, 10, 12–13, 37, 97,
129; musical education,
10–12, 34–5, 63, 70, 87,
115; becomes professional
musician, 13–17; starts
writing songs, 16; first
published works, 17, 20;
adopts Gershwin spelling,
17; piano style, 17, 32;
sense of humour, 22, 72;
and women, 24–5, 31, 71,
109, 137–8, 144; lifestyle,
25, 73, 76; association
with Dreyfus and Harms,
26, 35; earnings, 33, 56,
60, 87; indigestion, 42,
109, 139; first trip to Europe, 44–5; begins concert
hall career, 46; composition
and first performance of
Rhapsody in Blue, 49–55;
working habits, 61; tension
*between light and serious mu-
sic,* 68; relationship with Kay

*Swift Warburg, 70–1, 76,
97, 133, 135, 137; rift with
Whiteman, 74, 80; learns to
drive, 81; last trip to Europe,
85–91; describes ideal concert,
87; composition of An American in Paris, 90–3; moves
into own home, 95–7; and
interior design, 2, 96, 133;
confidence, 97; sues Ziegfeld,
99; conducting debut, 99,
102–3; interest in opera,
100–1; method of collaboration, 102; and Frankie's
marriage, 106; in Hollywood,
107–8, 133, 135, 137–41,
143–4; enthusiasm for
recording technology, 108–9;
publishes George Gershwin's
Song Book, 114; ignores
Langley's accusation, 116;
Music by Gershwin radio
programme, 122; composition
and first performances of Porgy
and Bess, 118–31; undergoes
therapy, 132; illness, 139,
141, 143–6; affair with
Paulette Goddard, 141,
143–4; failure to marry,
144; death, 146; funeral,
147; dies intestate, 147*

*FILMS: A Damsel in Dis-
tress, 138, 140–1; Delicious,
107–9; The Goldwyn Follies,
141, 143; Shall We Dance,
137–8, 140*

*INSTRUMENTAL
WORKS: An American in
Paris, 86, 88, 90–3, 94–5,
99, 112, 137; Catfish Row,
132; Concerto in F, 2, 64–8,
78, 88, 131, 139; Cuban
Overture, 116; Five Preludes,
78, 147; Lullaby, 34, 42;
Manhattan Rhapsody, 107;
Porgy and Bess orchestral
suite, 132; Rhapsody in
Blue, 1, 2, 49–56, 59, 63,
65, 68, 74, 78, 79–81,*

86, 88, 94, 99, 106, 112, 115, 121, 131, 147; *Rialto Ripples,* 17, 20; *Rumba,* 115–16; *Second Rhapsody,* 108–9, 111–14; *Short Story,* 78; *Sleepless Night,* 79; *Variations on 'I Got Rhythm',* 121

OPERAS: 135th Street, 71; Blue Monday, 42–3, 47, 71; *Porgy and Bess,* 1, 43, 118–31, 132, 147; *Song of the Flame,* 62, 63, 67, 72

SHOWS: *Black-Eyed Susan,* 56–7; *East Is West,* 98, 103; *Funny Face,* 84–5, 86, 89; *Girl Crazy,* 103–5; *Lady, Be Good!,* 58–60, 62, 73–5, 82, 83, 105; *La-La Lucille!,* 28–30, 32, 35, 40; *Let Them Eat Cake,* 117, 118; *Mayfair,* 75–6; *Of Thee I Sing,* 108, 110–12, 114, 117; *Oh, Kay!,* 71, 76–7, 81, 83, 86; *Pardon My English,* 109, 114, 116, 117; *The Perfect Lady,* 47; *Primrose,* 56, 58, 59; *The Rainbow,* 44; *Rosalie,* 85, 86; *Scandals,* 25, 35–6, 40–5, 55–6, 71; *Show Girl,* 98–9, 103; *Smarty,* 83–4; *Strike Up the Band,* 1, 81–2, 83–4, 90, 101–3, 117; *Sweet Little Devil,* 47, 49; *Tell Me More,* 62; *Tip-Toes,* 62, 63, 67, 71, 83; *Treasure Girl,* 90, 93–4, 103

SONGS: *'All to Myself',* 41; *'Buzzard Song',* 130; *'Come to the Moon',* 30; *'Do It Again',* 46; *'Embraceable You',* 2, 105, 114, 131; *'Fascinating Rhythm',* 2, 58, 60, 114; *'A Foggy Day',* 140; *Four Tunes,* 116; *'I Got Rhythm',* 2, 104–5, 131; *'I'll Build a Stairway to Paradise',* 36, 43; *'Isn't It a Pity?',* 116; *'It Ain't Necessarily So',* 126; *'I've Got a Crush on You',* 93, 103; *'Lady, Be Good!',* 60; *'Let's Call the Whole Thing Off',* 135; *'Making of a Girl',* 20; *'The Man I Love',* 58, 73, 77, 82, 85; *'My Runaway Girl',* 20; *'Naughty Baby',* 57; *'Nice Work If You Can Get It',* 140; *'Nobody But You',* 30; *'O Land of Mine, America',* 28; *'Oh Do It Again',* 40–1; *'Our Love Is Here to Stay',* 143; *'Ragging the Traumerei',* 16; *'The Real American Folk Song (Is a Rag)',* 27–8; *'Sam and Delilah',* 105; *'Since I Lost You',* 16; *'Some Wonderful Sort of Someone',* 27; *'Somebody Loves Me',* 36, 56; *'Someone to Watch Over Me',* 77; *'Soon',* 103; *'Summertime',* 122, 130, 148; *'Swanee',* 2, 19, 31–4, 35, 44, 46, 148; *'Sweet and Low-Down',* 62; *'That Certain Feeling',* 62; *'They All Laughed',* 135; *'They Can't Take That Away From Me',* 137; *'Walking the Dog',* 137; *'What Love Has Done to Me',* 105; *'When You Want 'Em You Can't Get 'Em',* 17, 19, 20; *'You-oo Just You',* 24

Gershwin, Ira: birth, 5; childhood, 6; scholarly nature and love of reading, 7, 9, 37; learns piano, 8; leaves college, 19; writing as Arthur Francis, 27–8, 37–8, 40, 41; on George, 28–9, 37, 38–9; personality, 37; courtship, engagement and marriage, 37, 60, 81; on *Rhapsody in Blue,* 47, 49, 51, 56; begins writing under own name and with George, 57, 59–60; earnings, 60; working habits, 61; praised by Lorenz Hart, 62; drafted, 69; emergency appendectomy, 76; learns to drive, 81; lives near George, 95, 117, 135; known as 'the Jeweller', 102; method of collaboration, 102; and Frankie's marriage, 106; in Hollywood, 107–8, 135, 138, 140–1, 144–5; backs show, 111; wins Pulitzer Prize, 111; renames *Catfish Row,* 132; and George's illness, 145–6; seeks adjudication on Gershwins' work, 147

FILMS: *A Damsel in Distress,* 138, 140–1; *The Goldwyn Follies,* 141; *Shall We Dance,* 137–8

OPERA: *Porgy and Bess,* 120, 123–4, 131

SHOWS: *East Is West,* 98; *Follies of 1936,* 123; *Funny Face,* 84–5; *Girl Crazy,* 103; *Lady, Be Good!,* 59–60; *Let Them Eat Cake,* 117; *Of Thee I Sing,* 108, 110; *Oh, Kay!,* 70–1, 75–7; *Pardon My English,* 114, 116; *Show Girl,* 98–9; *Strike Up the Band,* 81–2, 102–3; *Treasure Girl,* 93–4

SONGS: *'The Babbitt and the Bromide',* 84;

'Fascinating Rhythm',
58, 60; 'A Foggy Day',
140–1; 'Isn't It a Pity?',
116; 'Let's Call the Whole
Thing Off', 135; 'Naughty
Baby', 57; 'Our Love Is
Here to Stay', 143; 'The
Real American Folk Song
(Is a Rag)', 27–8; 'Sleepless
Night', 79; 'Someone', 41;
'They All Laughed', 135;
'Tra-La-La', 41; 'Two Lit-
tle Girls in Blue', 40

Gershwin, Lenore (Lee)
(née Strunsky), 40, 61,
97, 106; courtship,
engagement and mar-
riage, 37, 60, 81; trip
to Europe, 85; lives near
George, 117, 135; and
George's illness, 141,
143, 145–6
Gilbert and Sullivan, 82,
110
Gilman, Lawrence, 54
Glaenzer, Jules, 40–1,
44, 66
Glazunov, Alexander, 115
Gluck, Alma, 48
Glyndebourne, 131
Goddard, Paulette, 141,
143–4
Godowsky, Frances, see
Gershvin, Frances
Godowsky, Leopold, Jr, 89,
90, 138; marriage, 95,
106–7
Goetz, E Ray, 41
Goldberg, Isaac, 49, 102,
105, 107, 108
Goldfarb, Mr, 11
Goldmark, Rubin, 34
Goldwyn, Sam, 133, 141,
143
Goodman, Benny, 105
Gorman, Ross, 49, 53,
80, 88
Gorn, Isadore, 78
Green, Miss, 10
Greenberg, Rodney, 43

Grofé, Ferde, 41, 49, 51,
63, 97
Gullah people, 119, 122
Gumble, Mose, 15–16,
19, 21

Half-Past Eight, 26
Hambitzer, Charles,
11–12, 13, 34, 35
Hammerstein, Oscar, II,
23, 67, 120
Harburg, Yip, 19, 145
Harms, T B, 15, 25–6, 35
Harris, Sam, 114
Hart, Edward, 78
Hart, Lorenz, 62
Haymon, Cynthia, 131
Hearst, William Randolph,
23
Heifetz, Jascha, 48, 54, 64,
66, 70
Heifetz, Pauline, 64, 67–8
Herald Tribune, 48
Herbert, Victor, 22, 28,
51, 54
Heyward, Dorothy, 118,
119, 123
Heyward, DuBose,
118–20, 122–3, 125–6,
131, 147
Hindemith, Paul, 45
'Hindustan', 31
Hitler, Adolf, 117
Hollywood, 108–9, 133,
135, 137–8, 143–4
Houston Grand Opera,
131
Howard, Willie, 105
Hudson river, 95
Hutcheson, Ernest, 64, 65

interpolation, 20
Irish, 70

Jablonski, Edward, 1, 34,
71, 78, 84, 135, 144
Jackson, Arthur, 29, 36
Jaffe, Max, 45
jazz, 41–5, 46, 48, 54, 60,
66, 91, 119
Jazz Age, 2, 68

Jews, 4, 10, 54, 70
Jolson, Al, 32–3, 94, 98,
120
Joplin, Scott, 119

Kahn, Gus, 99
Kahn, Otto, 47, 56, 58
Kalman, Emmerich, 89
Kaufmann George S, 81–2,
101–2, 108–11, 117, 139
Kaye, Danny, 10
Kearns, Allan, 105
Keeler, Ruby, 94, 98
Kelly, Gene, 84, 92
Kent, Duke of, 56, 60
Kent, William, 105
Kern, Eva, 23
Kern, Jerome, 12, 20, 22,
27, 45, 48, 140; biog-
raphy, 22; encourages
Gershwin, 23–5; cooling
with Gershwin, 29; Porgy
project, 120; Gershwin's
neighbour, 135
Kilenyi, Edward, 12, 13,
34, 99
klezmer music, 2, 10, 43
Kodak Company, 95
Kolisch, Rudolf, 89
Koussevitzky, Serge, 110,
111–12
Krupa, Gene, 105

La Scala, 131, 147
Ladies First, 27
Lane, Burton, 35
Langley, Allan, 116
Lannin, Paul, 41
Lawrence, Gertrude, 75–7,
83, 86, 90, 93–4, 107
Lawrence, Vincent, 94
Lehár, Franz, 89
'Les Six', 90
Levant, Oscar, 27, 68, 111,
115, 143–4, 146
Levy, Paul, 145
London, 57, 59, 62, 75,
83, 85; Gershwin in, 44,
56, 73–4, 79, 86; post-
war, 69
Long Branch, NJ, 82

Lopez, Vincent, 48
Los Angeles, 133, 138–9, 144–7

McCormack, John, 40
MacDonald, Ballard, 56
MacDonald, Jeanette, 62
McEvoy, J P, 99
McGowan, John, 103
Mamoulian, Rouben, 63, 124, 128, 129
'mammy' songs, 14, 31, 32
Manners, Margaret, see Charleston, Mollie
Marx, Chico, 21
Marx, Groucho, 24
Marx Brothers, 102
Mason, Daniel Gregory, 46
Maxwell, Elsa, 89
Meadows, Ralph, 126
Merman, Ethel, 103–5
Metropolitan Opera, 101, 118
Mexico, 108, 132
Milhaud, Darius, 45
Miller, Glenn, 105
Miller, Jack, 11
Miller, Marilyn, 85
Miller, Mitch, 139
Miss 1917, 22–3, 25, 35
Modigliani, Amedeo, 72
Mosbacher, Emil, 123
Mountbatten, Lady, 73
Mozart, Wolfgang Amadeus, 87
Mueller, Paul, 143, 145
Musical America, 51, 90
Musicians' Symphony Orchestra, 116

Naffziger, Dr Howard C, 146
Nathan, George Jean, 85, 111
New Music Review, 46
New York, 2, 4, 10, 60, 69–70, 100, 112, 133; portrayed in Rhapsody in Blue, 53

LOCATIONS: 33
Riverside Drive, 95,

97, 103–4, 117; 44th Street Theater, 72; 103rd Street, 60–1, 63–4, 72, 73, 81; 132 East 72nd Street, 117, 123; Aeolian Hall, 45, 52–3, 55; Alvin Theater, 84–5, 94, 105, 129; Brooklyn, 5, 7; Capitol Theater, 30, 32; Carnegie Hall, 24, 45, 55, 65, 66, 71, 93, 112, 114; Century Theater, 24; Fox's City Theater, 21–2; Globe Theater, 65, 66; Grand Central Station, 69; Harlem, 2, 42; Juilliard School, 64; Lewisohn Stadium, 99, 114, 115–16, 132; Liberty Theater, 71, 73; Liederkrantz Hall, 79–80; Lower East Side, 2, 4, 33; Manhattan, 8, 9, 26, 53, 81, 95; Park Avenue, 40; Temple Emanuel, 147; Times Square, 30; Winter Garden, 20, 32
New York Philharmonic Orchestra, 88, 90, 99
New York Symphonic Society, 63, 93
New York Times, 67, 77, 93, 111, 116, 130
Newark, NJ, 67, 135, 145
Nichols, Red, 105
Novello, Ivor, 69
Nunn, Trevor, 131

O'Hara, John, 1
opera, 100–1, 118–19
Osgood, Henry, 51
Ossining, NY, 81

Paley, Herman, 18, 24, 37–40, 52, 146
Paley, Lou, 18, 24, 30, 37–40, 52, 146
Pallay, George, 109, 114, 144, 146
Paris, 44, 69, 72, 74, 86–91

Passing Show of 1916, The, 20
Perfection Studios, 16–17
Perkins, Edward B, 26
Perrett, Geoffrey, 42
Peyser, Joan, 133, 139
Philadelphia, 58, 59, 67, 85, 93, 132
piano rolls, 16–17, 20, 148
Pianola, 16–17
Picasso, Pablo, 72
Pittsburgh, 27
pluggers, 14–15
popular music, 12, 14–16, 19, 45, 60
Porter, Cole, 89
Praskins, Leonard, 16
Pringle, Aileen, 108
Prohibition, 77, 94
Prokofiev, Sergei, 87, 90

ragtime, 16, 27, 28, 29, 46, 66
Rakhmaninov, Sergei, 48, 66
Rand, Dr Carl, 146
Random House, 114
Ravel, Maurice, 45, 86, 87
Reiner, Fritz, 132
Remick's (Jerome H Remick & Company), 15–20, 24, 31, 75, 121, 141
Rettenberg, Milton, 56
Revue des Ambassadeurs, La, 89, 90
revues, 36
RKO Pictures, 11, 133, 138
Robeson, Paul, 125
Rock-a-Bye Baby, 25
Rodgers, Richard, 62
Rogers, Ginger, 22, 103, 105, 133, 135, 138
Romberg, Sigmund, 20, 21, 85
Ronnell, Ann, 131
Rosanka, Josefa, 89
Rosen, Max, 7–8, 40
Roth, Murray, 19–20
Rouault, Georges, 72
Russia, 4
Ryskind, Morrie, 101–2,

108–11, 117

St Louis, 55
San Francisco, 138
Sanborn, Pitts, 54
Sandow, Hyman, 92
Scandinavians, 70
Schillinger, Joseph, 115, 124
Schirmer, Mabel, 74–5, 86–7, 90, 97, 144, 147; Gershwin's letters to, 137–8, 141, 143
Schirmer, Robert, 74, 86
Schneider, Alan, 64
Schoenberg, Arnold, 45
Schwartz, Arthur, 76
Seattle, 138
Segal, Vivienne, 23–4
Selwyn, Edgar, 82, 90, 101
Sheehan, Winford, 107
sheet music, 14, 30, 32, 33, 34, 114
Shelter Island, 123
Shilkret, Nathaniel, 11, 80, 99; records *An American in Paris,* 94–5
'shouting', 122–3
Show Boat, 82
Siegel, Jeffrey, 65, 147
Simmel, Dr Ernest, 144
Simon, Simone, 137
Sinbad, 32–3
slaves, 28, 29, 43
Smallens, Alexander, 125
Smith, Queenie, 62
Sondheim, Stephen, 34, 82, 102
songwriters, 14–15
Soudekeine, Serge, 125
Sousa, John Philip, 54
South Carolina, 118, 119, 123, 126
Southampton, 44
spirituals, 28, 46, 122
Stein, Gertrude, 130
Steinert, Alexander, 125, 128–9
Stevens, George, 141
Stokowski, Leopold, 87
Strauss, Johann, 89

Strauss, Richard, 87, 92
Stravinsky, Igor, 54, 87
Strayhorn, Billy, 41
Strunsky, Leonore (Lee), *see* Gershwin, Leonore
Swift, Kay, *see* Warburg, Kay Swift
Syracuse, NY, 26

Taylor, Bert, 107
Taylor, Deems, 46, 91
Teagarden, Jack, 105
That's Entertainment, 84
Theatre Guild, 118, 124, 125, 129
Thompson, Fred, 58, 83, 94
Thomson, Virgil, 125, 130
Tin Pan Alley, 14, 16, 19, 21, 24, 25, 30, 34
Tiomkin, Dimitri, 90
'trunk' songs, 29, 44, 65, 85, 93, 98, 107
Tucker, Sophie, 19

Urban, Joseph, 23, 99
Utrillo, Maurice, 72

van Vechten, Carl, 45, 51
Variety, 26, 33
Verdi, Giuseppe, 131
Victor Recording Company, 108
Victor Talking Machine Company, 79–80
Vienna, 89
Vodery, Will, 19, 21
von Tilzer, Harry, 15, 20

Wall Street Crash, 81, 99, 100
Wallace, Edgar, 44
Walling, Rosamund, 109–10
Warburg, Edward, 132
Warburg, James Paul, 70, 133
Warburg, Kay Swift, 68, 81, 89, 93, 141, 147; relationship with Gershwin, 70–1, 76,

97, 133, 135, 137; and Gershwin's home, 95; and Frankie Gershwin's marriage, 107; dedicatee of *Song Book,* 114; and *Porgy and Bess,* 124, 129; introduces Gershwin to psychiatrist, 132; divorced, 133, 135; working at Radio City Music Hall, 143
Washington, DC, 67
Wayburn, Ned, 31–2
Weill, Kurt, 89
Whistler, J A M, 52
White, George, 23, 25, 35, 42–3; *Scandals,* 25, 35–6, 40–5, 55–6, 71
White, Willard, 131
Whiteman, Paul, 41–2, 45, 47, 59, 71, 97; *What Is American Music?,* 48, 52–3, 55; records *Rhapsody in Blue,* 56, 79–80; London debut, 74; *'The King of Jazz',* 74, 80; rift with Gershwin, 74, 80; *King of Jazz* film, 80–1
Whiting, Richard, 36
William Tell Overture, 11
Wilmington, Delaware, 67
Wodehouse, P G, 22, 71, 77, 85, 140
Wolpin, Kate Bruskin, 8, 10
Woolcott, Alexander, 79
World War One, 33, 68, 81
World War Two, 81, 100

Youmans, Vincent, 40

Ziegfeld, Florenz, 23, 35, 75, 85, 98–9; bankruptcy, 99; *Follies,* 31, 36, 123
Zilboorg, Gregory, 132
Zimbalist, Efrem, 48
Zimmerman, Ethel, *see* Merman, Ethel
Zoltai, Stephan, 124